"Sex doesn't make anyone into a woman!"

Tara said fiercely, her eyes angry now, the dreamy magic gone.

"The knowledge of her sexual power does," Ben asserted. "You've never recognized yours. When it hits you, you go overboard. Next time you might not be so lucky."

"You certainly don't want me," Tara blazed, shame filling her as she realized what she'd said. "And I certainly don't want you," she added wildly.

His eyes narrowed on her face, the tight anguish of her body.

"I like my women to be mature," he said softly. "I like them to know exactly what they're getting into. As to your afterthought—ask yourself why you always fight me, avoid looking at me, why you take to your heels whenever possible. The answers should make you a lot older and wiser."

PATRICIA WILSON used to live in Yorkshire, England, but with her children all grown up, she decided to give up her teaching position there and accompany her husband on an extended trip to Spain. Their travels are providing her with plenty of inspiration for her romance writing.

Books by Patricia Wilson

HARLEQUIN PRESENTS

HARLEQUIN ROMANCE

Don't miss any of our special offers. Write to us at the following address for information on our newest releases.

Harlequin Reader Service
901 Fuhrmann Blvd., P.O. Box 1397, Buffalo, NY 14240
Canadian address: P.O. Box 603,
Fort Erie, Ont. L2A 5X3

PATRICIA WILSON

guardian angel

Harlequin Books

TORONTO • NEW YORK • LONDON
AMSTERDAM • PARIS • SYDNEY • HAMBURG
STOCKHOLM • ATHENS • TOKYO • MILAN

Harlequin Presents first edition April 1990
ISBN 0-373-11262-9

Original hardcover edition published in 1989
by Mills & Boon Limited

CHAPTER ONE

TARA looked up and tensed in annoyance. She had no real idea why Ben Shapiro angered her so much. There wasn't a thing about him that she could point to and criticise in all fairness, but the thought that at any moment he would step into her office and speak to her had every nerve in her body on edge.

As an employer he was wonderful—too good to be true, in fact. Since her father's death in the dreadful accident that had left her mother paralysed, he had been like a godfather. It made her feel guilty that, in spite of his goodness, she detested him. Correction! He irritated her, wound her up.

It was his manner, probably. As head of the giant Internationl Science Technology he was naturally powerful, often remote, certainly brilliantly clever, but there was no need for him to be so assertively masculine. That was where the heart of her resentment really rested.

He was standing just outside her door, talking to Bob Carter of Personnel, and she sat there almost chewing her nails, like a twenty-four-year-old schoolgirl, hoping he would go right on and not come in. She found herself watching him surreptitiously, disgusted as she realised she had crossed her fingers. Every meeting with him was fraught with difficulty, and suppressed annoyance on her part as she tried to come up with some explanation of why he managed to. make her feel inadequate.

He was tall, his hair almost black, thick and inclined to wave. His face was always filled with a kind of arrogant amusement when he wasn't downright angry, although he rarely lost his temper, he was too clever for that. He got the best out of everyone, even her! It was his eyes, she decided, clear topaz, filled with irony, his lashes so dark and thick she could see them from here. And he *was* going to come in!

The phone rang and she pounced on it gladly, an excuse to avoid looking up.

'Tara Frost,' she said pleasantly.

'Oh, Miss Frost, there's a call for you on line one.'

She pressed the switch and spoke in her clear voice, 'music to the ear', her father used to say.

'Good afternoon. Tara Frost, Public Relations. Can I help you?'

'My dear Tara, you already have, the Kadinese Republic is for ever in your debt!'

The cultured voice of Patrick Ndele came over the phone as clearly as if he were in the room, and Tara's face lit up with a smile. Ben Shapiro walked in at that moment, and she glanced up but made the most of her excuse to avoid looking at him.

'Patrick, how lovely to hear from you! We had all the reports. I was so relieved to know that everything was back to normal, and don't thank me, it was the firm. IST is always ready to help out.'

She couldn't help glancing up then, and Ben Shapiro's lips were quirking in amusement, his golden eyes acknowledging that she did her job very well. It annoyed her instantly. It was patronising!

'Meeting!' he said clearly, seeing her annoyance

and ignoring it. She looked away and went on talking.

'Yes. Whenever you're in London I'd love to see you!'

Ben Shapiro's hand came out in front of her face, his eyes now a little annoyed at her lack of respect in ignoring his presence. The hand opened and made a sharp, hard jab at the air. Five minutes! She nodded offhandedly and he walked out, his winged brows drawn together in a frown, and Tara quickly ended the conversation, beginning to gather her notes and files. When he said five minutes, he meant exactly that. If she was late she would get the edge of that sarcastic tongue, and she wasn't going to give him the satisfaction!

She wished heartily that she didn't dislike him so much. It would have been much more comfortable to dote on him. Her life had changed so much over the past six months, one shock after another, and throughout it all the firm had stood by her, supporting her, and the firm meant Ben Shapiro.

There had been nothing but happiness in her life until that cruel, snowy night when a freak accident had taken the life of her father and left her mother paralysed. The driver of the lorry their car had hit had been too shocked to speak much at the time, but he had managed to get help, although it had been too late for her father. Her mother had been unconscious and later remembered very little except the lights that suddenly came at them, the awesome noise of the crash.

Tara had been in a late meeting when the news had been brought in by a white-faced secretary, and it had stunned her into immobility. It had been Ben Shapiro

who had acted, Ben who had taken care of her, closing
the meeting and taking her to the hospital, and for the
next few days seeing to everything, every minute,
heartbreaking detail that made things like that more
painful still.

Her mother thought he was Mr Wonderful, and
Tara had been so grateful that she had almost got to
the stage where she could not act without his
approval. It was that which finally alerted her to the
danger of a man like that. She was not about to
succumb to the weak-female act. She was now the one
stable prop in her mother's life, and she had a very
demanding job too. She had stiffened up and taken the
reins firmly back into her own hands, refusing further
offers of help.

Almost late! She ran a comb through her hair and
hurried along the corridor to the conference room.
She was slight, not at all tall, almost boyish, but her
figure had lovely singing lines, her willowy
slenderness disguising great vigour and determination. Her face was unusual, her eyes extremely dark
against the pale, shining blonde of her hair, hair that
was cut in a thick bob, curving around her face, the
thick fringe drawing attention to those unusual
slanting, dark eyes. 'A fascinating little cat,' Martin
called her. It was a relief to know he would be at the
meeting. He had flown in from Brazil this morning
and she hadn't even seen him yet.

His was the first face she saw as she opened the
door, and his broad wink had her smile winging to
him across the long, heavy, polished table as she slid
into her place.

'Right! Now that the female brains have arrived,

we'll begin!' Ben Shapiro's cool, sardonic voice made her hackles rise at once, but her irritated glance was lost on him and she caught the eye of his secretary, Joan, who made a face and joined her in a silent feminine conspiracy. She simmered down.

'As you no doubt notice,' he remarked coolly, his sardonic amusement dying away completely as business began, 'Lambourne is back from Brazil. You'll all get notes of my meeting with him, but the basic point is that the new Firmino drug is in the bag. We have the patents and it will be licensed out for development next month. Everything is set up.' He shot a look at Tara. 'Do you speak Portuguese?'

'No,' she said quickly. 'Anyway, Martin has Brazil, he speaks Portuguese.'

'He's not Public Relations!' Ben Shapiro reminded her coldly, looking slightly irked that she was trying to avoid upsetting Martin. 'Anything blows up there, and you'll be needed. You don't speak Portuguese? Learn it!'

'Will tomorrow be soon enough?' Tara asked pertly, but he ignored her, ploughing on with the rest of the business.

He always took her breath away. She had plenty of energy herself, but his driving-power made her feel weak. Chairman of International Science Technology, he had built it up to what it was now, it was almost his brainchild, and he knew every last detail about each part of it; nothing escaped his attention, nobody escaped the flash of those topaz eyes.

This room was a sort of reverse brain drain, like a black hole, sucking in the latest scientific ideas, the best brains. She sometimes asked herself how she had got here, but Ben Shapiro had made that quite plain when her probationary time had been up and he had promoted her straight to her present post in Public Relations. He only employed the best, and she had the potential to be just that. His opinion had made her glow and she had always worked hard, enjoying it; she still did. She spoke several languages, three of them fluently, and it was largely through her services and charm that business came their way.

Every big idea in the scientific field, every innovation, was gathered by this firm. Ben Shapiro knew that not all commercially viable scientific ideas came from the western world. Education in the developing countries was improving in leaps and bounds, and it was almost as important for them to have their own research as to have an army. An increasing number of ideas came from the Third World, and scientists heading laboratories there had come from advanced research centres in Britain, America and the continent.

IST signed deals with the government of the day in the new countries, getting worldwide control of patents, licensing them out in the developed world for manufacture and refining. The percentage that the country of origin got was large. The percentage to IST was small but, with a potential market of billions stretching into the foreseeable future, it was big business at the top of the range.

'How are we getting on with the new Medane research?' Ben was asking sharply at the end of the meeting when all reports had been read and Tara had thankfully finished hers, his eyes cool and golden on Bryan Wainwright. 'Mepacrine is old hat now. The

African countries need a new drug against malaria, and this looks like being it. Apart from their needs,' he added sarcastically, 'there's a goldmine in this. We're not talking peanuts! Tara practically put this in your lap with her work in Kadina and the way she got on with Patrick Ndele!'

Tara stiffened, glaring at him, but he was too busy glaring at Bryan Wainwright to notice her disapproval. He had no right to hold her up as an example to anyone. The job she did was entirely different from Bryan's. It was a pleasure and a privilege to do her job, and she knew that Bryan was sometimes a bit slow off the mark. He would get the chop if he didn't move faster. She didn't want to be involved with that sort of thing.

'Can I speak to you?' she said coldly to Ben as the meeting broke up.

Ben Shapiro looked up sharply at her tone, handing his papers and files to Joan.

'Second sight!' he said mockingly. 'I was just about to say the same thing to you. My office,' he finished briefly, standing back politely to see her out.

'Seven o'clock, Tara?' Martin said as he passed, his hand just touching her hair in an intimate and possessive manner that she wished he wouldn't use at work.

She nodded, smiling, and couldn't help glancing at Ben Shapiro. He looked down his nose at her coldly, and then his lips quirked in that irritating way as he ushered her into the office and indicated the seat opposite his desk.

'You wanted to see me. I wanted to see you,' he said evenly. 'I'll give you first bite.'

He had an annoying way of putting things, too, Tara noticed. It was really alarming how she had begun to get annoyed with him so readily. She couldn't remember feeling like that before. It should have been entirely the opposite since her father's death. There had been a time when she had seemed to be on really good terms with him, and then every instinct had warned her of his domineering attitude. Since then she had felt a great antagonism towards him, doubly so because it made her feel guilty.

'It's unlikely that you came in here to advise me to change my tie!' he said mockingly as she came back to the present with a snap and realised she had been staring at him for the past few seconds.

'It's about Bryan Wainwright,' Tara said sharply, her face flushing under his probing stare. 'I really wish you wouldn't make remarks like that!'

'I run this firm my way!' he replied forcefully, his eyes no longer mocking. 'My heads of department have authority, budget control, personnel control and an entirely free hand, so long as they come up with the goods. They have top pay and top facilities. I expect action, and if I don't get it I stamp on toes. I haven't stamped on your toes yet—pussycat!'

Tara gasped. He had never spoken to her like that before! Her mouth opened and closed again in outrage.

'If—if you're trying to set off one employee against another . . .' she began, deciding to ignore the personal comment.

'I'm trying to run a multi-million-pound business!' he said briskly. 'I play it by ear. Now, if you've finished with the complaints, let's get to important matters. I want you to go out to Omari.'

'No!' Tara looked at him stubbornly, and he sat down slowly, tipping his chair back and regarding her with narrowed eyes.

'We'll begin again, because I didn't hear that,' he said softly, his whole attitude menacing. 'Your job is to go where you're needed, to charm the birds out of the trees, to use your language skills, help people who need us and leave behind goodwill. I want you in Omari by Monday at the latest.'

He didn't look at all like the man who had just made a very personal remark. He looked exactly what he was: a clever, hard-headed businessman who had power and knew how to use it.

'I can't go,' she said a little desperately. 'I want to go, but I can't leave now.'

'You mean because Martin Lambourne has only just got back?' he bit out angrily.

'No!' He was making her feel idiotic. Why didn't he just keep quiet and let her speak? 'I like going out to other countries. I like doing what I do, it's exciting.'

'More exciting than Lambourne? I'm intrigued,' he said mockingly, his eyes still cold.

'It's my mother,' said Tara in sudden desperation, blushing under the intensity of the cold stare. 'I can't leave her just now.'

He let his chair drop slowly on to its four legs and leaned back, his hands in his pockets.

'You left her to go to Kadina,' he said quietly. 'Why not now?'

'It was a bit of a risk,' Tara answered softly, looking away. 'My cousin came to stay for the short time I was away. It—it didn't work out.'

'Why?' His eyes were probing again, lancing over her, wheedling out her thoughts, and she suddenly held her head up and faced him head on.

'My cousin is a model, actress and . . . this and that! She didn't like looking after an invalid and I'll not ask her again!'

'Hmm.' Ben Shapiro sat and looked at her keenly. 'This won't do at all.'

'Then fire me. Give me the sack!' Tara snapped, jumping up and glaring at him. 'I'm not leaving my mother until I can come up with a good arrangement. She doesn't like to have strangers taking care of her. It—it's embarrassing being incapable of doing things for yourself, and I'll not let her suffer the indignity. So, fire me!'

He stood up too, towering over her of course even from behind his desk, looking down at her as if she was out of her mind.

'Never in a million years,' he said softly. 'My dear child, you make the wheels turn, you're indispensable!'

'Oh!' Tara was stunned, her legs suddenly weak, and she sat down abruptly. He came round the desk, however, and collected her things, putting them under his arm and reaching down to collect her too.

'We can't manage without you, and although I can send somebody else this once, I'll be expecting trouble all the time. However, I see your dilemma. I have the beginnings of an idea. Get off home now and see to Miriam. I'll collect you for dinner and we'll work out the idea and see if it amounts to anything.'

'I—I've got a dinner date,' Tara said uneasily, remembering Martin's words as he'd left the meeting, but anxious now not to antagonise the boss.

'Break it!' he said evenly, his hand firm on her arm as he led her out. 'I'll pick you up at seven. Business before pleasure, Miss Frost!'

She couldn't think of a way out of it and, in any case, if he could come up with an idea then she wanted to hear it, but he was *not* taking over her affairs again!

Martin was waiting in her office when she got back, and he was not amused at her news.

'I've been away for weeks!' he complained heatedly. 'The first night back and Shapiro grabs you! I would have thought he got enough work out of you during office hours without slave-driving after work.'

'It's not really office business,' Tara said uneasily. 'I—I've got a personal problem and he's going to help, I think.'

'Pulling you back under his wing again, is he?' Martin rasped. 'I thought you'd realised his ability to work us to death here and step into our lives and manage our private affairs, too.'

That was not fair at all. As far as Tara knew he had never done anything of the sort. IST was a very benevolent firm that gave its expertise free to the Third World countries. It rose to the occasion whenever there was a disaster. The trucks and Land Rovers that sped across the world and were caught on TV in out of the way places, 'IST' across their sides, were such a normal sight that they went almost unnoticed. She should know, it was part of her job to arrange this help. The same concern was extended to the staff. If Martin had ever been in trouble as she had, he would have been glad of Ben Shapiro's unflagging energy.

'That's not true!' she said sharply. 'He helps anyone. I've never noticed him stepping into your life.'

'I'm not a cuddly little blonde!' Martin said nastily, and Tara's temper erupted.

'I do a very important job here and it has nothing to do with my sex! Let's compare salaries! I've never had to put up with sexual harassment, and I'm not going to start now. Nobody owns me. If that's your attitude, then . . .'

'Hold it! Hold it!' Martin started to laugh and pulled her into his arms, his eyes filled with amusement at her fiery temper. 'I know your value and so does Shapiro. I didn't miss the dig he got in at Bryan Wainwright. Put my unusually chauvinistic attitude down to disappointment. I wanted to see you myself, but I expect that the boss takes first place,' he finished with a sigh. 'What's your problem, anyway?'

'I thought you'd never ask!' Tara said with a sharp thread of sarcasm that had him looking rueful. 'As a matter of fact, he wants me in Omari by Monday, and I told him that I can't leave Mirry.'

'I'm astonished he didn't sack you on the spot. There's been a dam burst there, hundreds of people homeless. He'll want our people out at once. What's wrong with leaving your mother with that Janet person?'

'That Janet person is merely a next-door neighbour!' Tara said irritably. 'Popping in to look at Mirry during the day is one thing, staying to take care of her is entirely another. Janet is depressing, anyway. Ben knows that.'

'Oh, yes, I forgot that he's a friend of the family,' Martin grated. 'Of course he knows all the ins and outs.'

'He's only a friend of the family because he helped when it was needed,' Tara said sharply. 'It was before you joined the firm, so don't go basing assumptions on erroneous facts.'

'Jealousy!' Martin confessed ruefully.

'Of Ben Shapiro?' Tara looked at him in astonishment. 'He's the boss, and I don't know about you but he never lets me forget it!'

'The green-eyed monster takes no fact into consideration,' Martin said with a grin, pulling her back into his arms. 'I missed you, Tara.'

He gave her a long, satisfying kiss, and when she moved breathlessly away her eyes caught the cool, disgruntled look on Ben Shapiro's face as he walked by her office. Her face flushed painfully. There would be sarcastic words about that! Extraneous activities in office hours! She wished that she didn't have to meet him tonight.

In the event, he did not mention it. His manner was perfectly normal and he seemed to be determined that she enjoyed the meal and felt at her ease. Tara felt nothing of the sort. There was this uneasy feeling that he would at any time take her to task for allowing Martin into her office on matters that were not strictly business, and also a deep feeling of resentment that he was once again in a position to arrange things for her.

She didn't know what else to do, however, and a few minutes with Janet when she had arrived home had convinced her that this state of affairs could not continue. If she was to carry on with her job, demanding as it was, then some firm and final arrangement had to be made for Mirry. Tara could think of nothing, finances after all were fairly limited, in spite of her generous salary.

'Let's get to the matter in hand, then,' said Ben in a businesslike voice after Tara had eaten her way anxiously through two courses. 'The problem of Miriam.'

Everybody called her mother by her first name, including Tara. She had called her Mirry since she was small, but when he said it, it gave her a sort of shiver, as if he held some right to be in her family. She put her fork down and prepared to listen—warily.

'As far as I can see, Tara,' he said reasonably, 'it's not only the fact that you're frequently expected to go abroad, it's the day-to-day running of things, too. I expect full attention to work in working hours and I'm not so stupid that I fail to realise there are many times when your mind is back with your mother and not entirely on the business in hand.'

'If I've ever given you any reason to . . .' Tara began heatedly, but he held up his hand and stopped that instantly.

'Try not to be so prickly, child, and then we may get somewhere,' he said sharply. 'I'm trying to see things from your point of view. Believe me, I don't always bother.'

'I'm sorry.' Tara flushed and looked away, and heard his exasperated sigh before he continued.

'Let's get on, then!' he ordered briskly. 'I've been at your flat often enough to have summed Janet up. Frankly I find her a pain in the . . .'

Tara looked up in outrage, but he had not apparently intended to finish that remark and his grin caught her unexpectedly, forcing a reluctant smile to her face.

'Miriam is spirited and full of life, like her daughter,' he continued. 'I imagine that Janet's worst forebodings are not doing her any good at all.'

'No, Janet is—depressing,' Tara confided grimly.

'So what about an entirely new package?' said Ben quietly. 'A place where she'll be safe during the day and have her time well occupied, and a place where she can also be left in complete safety when you're out of the country.'

'Are you suggesting that I put Mirry into a nursing-home?' Tara asked loudly and irascibly, her dark eyes dangerously wide, her irate glance also taking in the waiter who was at that moment serving her favourite treacle tart.

'I'm suggesting nothing of the sort!' he said caustically, his dark brows threatening thunder to come. 'Thank you for imagining it.'

'I—I'm sorry,' Tara murmured, her rage subsiding.

'That's twice within the last few minutes you've expressed such regret!' he snapped. 'Don't you think it's time to control that temper and admit that you're not Supergirl? Everyone needs help from time to time, and all I'm doing is offering help, nothing more.'

'What—what did you have in mind?' Tara said warily, and he looked at her darkly, his own temper just under control.

'If the firm didn't need you so much——' he threatened softly. He appeared to be thinking that one over, and Tara sipped her wine anxiously, worried now at her attitude to this powerful man, admitting that she almost got away with murder with him. She couldn't continue to do so. She was not really indispensable, nobody was that!

'Do you know where I live?' he suddenly shot at her, and when she shook her head, mystified by the question, he looked at her steadily for a minute and then said, 'I have a house a few miles out of the city. A big house on a small country estate. I commute daily. It's not too hard, the motorway makes it almost as easy as forcing my way through the rush-hour traffic.'

'Are—are you suggesting that—that I—we live . . .?' Tara began, her face bright with embarrassment.

He gave a bark of laughter, his handsome head thrown back.

'I am not!' he said with amused eyes on her bright face. 'What a scenario! My dear Miss Frost, will you consent to live with me? I guarantee to take care of your mother!'

Tara didn't know where to look and he was suddenly very contrite, his strong hand covering her slender fingers across the table.

'My turn to apologise,' he said softly. 'You seem to bring out the devil in me. You're always jumping in with both feet. God knows how you manage to wind these foreign officials round your little finger. Or is it just me who gets the suspicion?'

In all fairness, she would have had to say yes, so she didn't answer that one at all, and he seemed to take the point because suddenly he was laughing again, his question left hanging in the air like a sword over her head.

'To allay your suspicions,' he said quietly, 'the house has a lodge. It's a small cottage at the entrance to the drive, well separated from the main house by the gounds and woodland. What I'm offering is for you to live there with Miriam.'

'But—but she'll be more isolated than ever!' Tara said in astonishment, her dark eyes scanning his face. 'At least here she has Janet.'

'In the village,' he continued, 'is a very nice person who is a retired nurse. She's sensible, chirpy, utterly reliable, and she's about Miriam's age. What I'm suggesting is that you hire her. She could come in daily on a normal basis and sleep in when you're away.'

'Money being no object?' Tara said, with a little glance of irritation at him. *He* was a millionaire, or so they said. She had no idea what the cost of a full-time nurse would be. There had to be saving each month in case Miriam ever needed anything.

'The lodge would be rent-free, as you're a member of the firm,' he said smoothly. 'If you sell the flat, which is in a very good area and probably worth ten times the value your father paid for it, you could invest that money and have plenty to spend on just about anything. You're well paid yourself.'

'Sell the flat?' Tara had never even thought of such a thing. They had lived there since she was a small girl, and although she had no doubt that it would now be worth a great deal, it would leave them both very vulnerable. 'I—I couldn't even think about selling the flat.'

'Why the hell not?' he said in sudden annoyance, and she bit her lip, looking carefully away from the probing amber stare.

'I—I suppose it's instinctive, built in. My father used to say that you should never take a job where your housing depended on it. He used to say that— that it makes you vulnerable to—to exploitation and . . .'

Even before he spoke she could feel the air vibrating with rage, but his voice was controlled, low.

'Correct me if I'm wrong,' he said tersely, 'but I imagine that I've just been insulted.'

Tara had not intended that at all, but she saw how it looked and could not meet his angry eyes. To apologise again seemed ludicrous, and she realised just how irritating she could be—had been.

'I—I didn't mean quite that . . .' she began quietly.

'Then what the hell did you mean?' he exploded. 'It seems to me, Miss Frost, that I'm taking welfare too far with you. I have better things to do with my time than to sit here trying to help you to keep your job and face your commitments. Obviously you do not need help. Certainly I do not need insults!'

He looked as if he was about to get up and walk off, and Tara was filled with wild feelings of remorse and panic.

'Please!' she said urgently. 'I really didn't mean to sound like that. Surely you realise that this is all so unexpected . . . I never dreamed that you were going to offer anything like that. No—nobody would be so—so generous! It took me by surprise. I suppose it quite frightened me.'

'Knowing as you do that I'm about to demand that you live with me as soon as I've got you and Miriam in my power?' he snapped corrosively.

'I—I didn't . . . I never . . .'

'I'm thirty-six, Miss Frost. Twelve years older and obviously twelve years wiser than you. I have women of my own! I do not need subterfuge to get anyone or anything!' He gave her a look of wild exasperation as she glanced up at him from beneath her blonde fringe. 'Oh, for God's sake, eat your treacle tart!' he rasped, sitting back and taking a great drink from his glass.

'I—I don't really want it now,' she began miserably, but he merely glared at her.

'Of course you do! You've been eyeing it longingly ever since that poor hapless waiter served it and got a red-hot glare from you. You've eaten your way through enough to sink a boat!' he added nastily. 'God knows where you put it all, you're like an underfed cat! I imagine it all goes up in temper.'

She made herself eat it and he glared at every mouthful until her hands were shaking. He was not about to speak to her again, apparently, and she saw, not for the first time, that he was powerful and ruthless. He was big, too; the hands that lay against the tablecloth were strong enough, big enough to snap her in two. He must have been reading her thoughts, because the long brown fingers began to beat an irritated tattoo on the white cloth.

'Decision! Now!' he suddenly rapped out.

'I'm very grateful. I really would like to discuss it with Mirry, though,' she got out anxiously, and was greatly relieved to see him nod in understanding.

'If she agrees,' he said in a calmer voice, 'then I suggest that you come up and see the place. Come tomorrow. It's Friday, and we can finish early. Come straight after work.'

'I'll have to bring Mirry,' Tara said quickly, and earned herself a further glare.

'Naturally!' he bit out. 'She's the one who will be there all the time. You'll be too busy working to get the full benefit of country living. I'll give you directions in the morning after you've spoken to her. I'll be shooting straight off after work. I'm having a visitor. No use waiting for you. I don't expect you to keep up with me.'

Not in any way at all, Tara thought ruefully, certainly not behind that bright red Ferrari. She was suddenly overwhelmed by her temerity in speaking to him as she sometimes did. He was right out of her class altogether. It was a miracle that she hadn't been fired months ago. She had better alter her ways. She loved her job. She looked up and gave him a lovely smile.

'Thank you for helping me, Mr Shapiro,' she breathed sweetly.

'A somewhat dubious pleasure, Miss Frost,' he said drily, one dark brow raised quizzically. 'Next time, pick on somebody your own size.' The topaz eyes flared over her derisively, and she vowed to do just that.

CHAPTER TWO

'ARE you all right?' Tara looked in the rear-view mirror and met the smiling gaze of her mother who was settled as comfortably as possible in the back seat of the car.

'I'm quite all right, Tara. It's rather like being in a coach, sitting here, hanging on to the strap, a rug over my legs and all this room.'

'Would you like to stop for a while? We have plenty of time.'

'Stop worrying, dear. I said that I'm all right and that's exactly what I am. Besides, I can hardly wait to get there! You can't possibly know how exciting this is for me!'

Tara smiled to herself. She knew when her mother was putting on a face. She never ceased to be proud of her mother's courage. So many people in her place would have simply given up, but not Miriam Frost! After the shock of the cruel accident there had been so many more shocks, one after another, and Tara had never heard one single word of complaint, and not one uselessly shed tear had clouded those bright eyes.

After weeks in hospital while Tara struggled to cope with the loss of her beloved father, the visiting, and her own work, her mother had been discharged into her care with the advice that she would never again be able to walk. Now she was settled in the back of Tara's car, the front passenger seat removed to give her more room, another of Ben Shapiro's ideas. He had wanted the firm to provide an estate car, but it was round about the time that Tara had begun to notice how her life was slowly being taken over, and she had refused. Anyway, 'the firm' had meant him.

'Not far now, Mirry. A few miles only and then we've reached the lodge.'

'How exciting it is, Tara, darling! I don't think that I've ever known a more generous man than Ben.'

'Yes,' Tara murmured, wondering why she felt so dubious about that. 'He's the most fabulous employer.'

She smiled to herself suddenly at the thought of Martin. Once again she had refused a dinner date, and he had been furious and suspicious about this venture.

'What exactly is Shapiro up to?' he had asked angrily, not even slightly mollified when she had explained the difficulties that faced her daily now that Mirry was almost helpless. 'He never makes a move without some plan at the back of it,' he had added, with a look at her as if she knew exactly which plan and was part of it.

'Obviously he doesn't like his staff to have worries,' Tara had said sharply, no more pleased with Martin's possessive attitude than she had been with Ben Shapiro's constant help.

'Fine! I'll tell him about my overdraft,' Martin sneered before he stormed off.

Men, apparently, were all alike. No, that wasn't quite true. Ben Shapiro was subtly different. Martin was very much bull-at-a-gate. She knew though that if she angered Ben too much he wouldn't hesitate to punish ferociously. It was a certain something about

him, the look in his eyes. He would never be
possessive about a woman. He was way, way above
that. And that was the basis of her constant irritation
with him she realised. He was superior.

'Thank you, Tara,' her mother said suddenly.
'Nobody could ever have a better daughter than you. I
know how hard you work. I know that your father is
proud of you, you're so alike.'

Momentarily, tears filled Tara's dark eyes, but she
blinked them away. Her mother spoke of her father as
if he were still alive, and it helped so much. It had
helped all through the time so far and it would go on
helping. It gave her the feeling of being blessed, as if
she always did the right thing, this trip included, in
spite of Martin's loudly spoken misgivings. It would
have been nice to have had some encouragement and
some help, so long as it hadn't been Ben Shapiro's
help.

'The first thing that you'll see, according to Ben's
instructions, will be Ellerdale Manor. Don't mistake
that for the lodge, otherwise you'll never recover from
the disappointment,' she said to her mother,
becoming aware that she had wrapped herself in her
private thoughts.

'I may be a city woman, Tara, dear, but I can tell a
manor from a lodge,' her mother laughed. 'How far
now?'

'Why? Are you in pain?' Tara said quickly, half
turning.

'No, I'm in an agony of suspense. I want to see it.'

'Soon, soon,' said Tara in amusement. 'You're too
impatient. I must have been spoiling you.'

The road was running beside a shallow stream, the

water bubbling over rounded stones, each gurgling ripple catching the sunlight. Tall old trees edged the side of the road, the scent of may-blossom filling the car, and as they rounded a bend Tara turned the car into a wide drive between two tall stone pillars, and across a brilliantly green meadow they saw a very old, very beautiful house.

'Ellerdale Manor,' said Tara, almost with a catch in her voice. She had not quite expected this, and in some weird way it scared her. It emphasised Ben Shapiro's wealth, his power and position. She had a sort of choking feeling, a trapped feeling, a wild hope surfacing that Mirry would hate the lodge. She didn't want to be so close to him, so much in his debt. Those ironic eyes hid a sort of danger that she could never quite place.

'It's magnificent!' her mother breathed in awe, her eyes on the manor.

'It's quite probably heaven,' Tara admitted before the woodland hid it from view. A very frightening guardian angel lived in that particular heaven. Seeing his home, imagining him away from the drive and dedication of the office, only made her instincts of self-preservation more sharp. Suddenly she wanted to turn the car and get out of there fast.

'Oh, Tara, it's lovely! I never expected anything like this.'

Tara snapped out of her small nightmare to realise tht they were at the lodge and that her mother was delighted. 'I was expecting to see a ruin, a run-down cottage with crumbling walls. I never expected to see this lovely place. It's quite big.'

Tara's eyes roamed over her mother's laughing face,

and she felt utterly trapped. She could never refuse her mother anything, never disappoint her. If Mirry liked it, she knew they would take Ben's offer.

'Did you imagine that Ben would have offered us a hovel?' she asked with more jollity than she felt. 'Don't get too excited until you see inside, though.'

Oh, let it be damp, dingy and miserable, she prayed silently. It was like putting her head into a noose, and no amount of self-deprecation could move that instinctive feeling.

'Right, out you come!' Tara opened the boot and got out the collapsible wheelchair that her mother used when they were out. She had learned by now how to manage the transfer from car to chair and back again, not that her mother was a big woman; like Tara she was slender and fine-boned. Even so she was a dead weight, and Tara had been forced to learn the knack of getting her in and out of places without relying on brute force.

'Look at the garden, Tara, it's beautiful!'

Tara could see that. The big garden was ablaze with spring flowers, with the brightness of the forsythia already aglow. Everything that was not blooming was in deep bud, and the smell of the old lilac tree filled the garden, the perfume mixing with the scent of may-blossom from the woods curving around the side of the house that faced Ellerdale Manor. A little spark of feeling quelled her misgivings. It was beautiful, after all.

Stone built, the same stone as the manor itself, mullioned windows winking in the sunlight, the lodge was very inviting. She pushed her mother up the path to the door, suddenly remembering that they could not see inside. She had not asked Ben for a key; come to think of it, he had never offered one!

'Tara, there's already a ramp! I'll be able to get in and out all by myself! Oh, Tara, Ben was so right! That man is clever beyond words, and kindness itself. I'll confess to you now, dear, that I hate Janet coming into the flat to see to me. I'll not need her any more if we put Ben's plan into action.'

Tara was standing looking at the ramp as if it were an evil manifestation. He had not had time to have this made since yesterday, even Ben Shapiro couldn't manage that, it was concrete. He had planned this weeks ago, maybe months. She felt like somebody in the bottom of a net.

She shook herself into action and peered through the windows, her face falling further at what she saw. Mirry was desperately wanting to see inside, too, but there was no way Tara could lift her. She would have to go to the manor and face Ben Shapiro to get the key. Mirry wouldn't understand if she didn't. It would have been a journey for nothing, and already her mother's heart was given to this place. She had lost a battle without firing one shot.

A voice from the end of the garden had her on edge more than ever. It was deeply dark and slightly amused; she knew the voice, she would have known it anywhere. Tara stiffened and then put on a smile, turning her head as Ben sauntered through the gate. Clearly he had walked down through the woods, and his timing was perfect. She had just had time to become dazed and scared. How typical!

He was not the Ben Shapiro of IST now, though; he was different, worse. The elegant business suit was discarded for black jeans and a black sweatshirt. His size, his physical power was more evident than ever, the sweatshirt sleeves pushed up to reveal strong forearms, the jeans tight across hard, lean hips.

Some sparkling gush of feeling shot through Tara as she remained perfectly still, her head half turned, staring at him as if he were unreal. He almost was, she mused. For the first time she realised just what he was, raw, handsome masculinity. A man that could devastate a woman. He had never looked more dangerous, more charming, and Mirry's face lit up with pleasure as she saw him. Tara's went pink. He noticed! He noticed everything. She stiffened with inner annoyance.

All Tara get was a pleasant nod, congratulations on her skill in map-reading, and then he ignored her, his whole attention given to her mother.

'You look well, Miriam,' he said gently. 'I haven't seen you for ages. As soon as you've looked at the lodge I'm going to capture you and take you up to the manor for tea.'

Ben Shapiro and her mother had a tendency to gush over each other, Tara noticed darkly, as he took a key from his pocket and opened the door. He took over the pushing of the chair too, wheeling Miriam inside and then leaving her to it. Tara let her mother look around by herself. She had already seen the interior through the windows, and she refused to make a show of interest while he was there.

The rooms that had probably been the old sitting-room and kitchen had been transformed into a bedroom with bathroom en suite, all planned for a disabled person, a woman, too, by the look of the colours. The room across the hall was a rather splendid sitting-room, a dining-extension with kitchen built on to the back of the lodge at one level. There was not a place here that would be beyond her mother's capabilites. At least some of her former competence could be restored, making her feel less of a burden. Tara swallowed her fears and suspicions and smiled happily, well aware of golden eyes on her expression face.

'This is *fabulous*, Tara!'

Miriam wheeled herself to the doorway and out into the blossoming garden, right down to the gate, as Tara leaned in the open doorway watching her mother's excitement.

'I see that you're not impressed,' said Ben quietly when her mother was out of hearing range.

'On the contrary, I'm quite stunned!' Tara answered evenly. She was not going to question him about this place with Mirry anywhere near, because there was going to be an almighty row. She could see that in his face.

'There's a bedroom and bathroom upstairs,' he said pointedly. 'Don't you want to see where you'll be putting your head at night?'

It sounded like a gibe at her for her suspicions when he had taken her to dinner to discuss this move, and Tara turned and went up the narrow stairs, staying as long as possible to avoid being alone with him. Very soon she was going to explode and she felt quite guilty about it.

Damn the man! She had always thought that Father Christmas was a bit sinister, the way he could get down chimneys and break into any room, and she couldn't help but feel that this magnificent generosity was sinister too, especially as he'd had it all prepared even before he had known that there was a problem. Mirry was so gullible, so trusting! She didn't seem to realise that not every lodge in the country was converted for a disabled woman.

'Well,' said Ben as Miriam wheeled her way back to the door, 'have you decided about my offer?'

'What do you think, darling? You haven't said much.'

'I was waiting for you to decide,' said Tara bravely. 'I don't want to influence you in any way.'

'Then we're coming, Ben, if you agree.' Her mother beamed at Ben Shapiro and Tara pulled down the flag, defeated by a bright smile and a wistful look.

'Well go up to the manor and celebrate with tea and cakes,' Ben declared, with a derisive look at Tara's well-controlled face. 'Will you drive up or walk?'

'We'll drive,' said Tara swiftly. And leave hastily, she added to herself. He didn't quibble, and she could hardly expect him to walk back when they were driving. He simply put Mirry into the car and took over, leaving Tara no option but to sit beside her mother.

It was a beautiful day and it gave her mother the chance to look around at the park as they went, to see the woodland at either side of the drive that led to the main house, and for them to get their first real look at Ellerdale Manor. Maybe Mirry would find something here that she could not face. She didn't.

'Oh, Tara, it's superb!' Her mother's voice echoed the awe that Tara felt when she saw the manor at close quarters.

The seventeenth-century house was built in traditional stone, mellow in the sunlight of the early afternoon, its beautiful proportions pleasing to the eye. The very look of the place had a calming effect on the nerves, and Tara sighed deeply, knowing her mother's romantic nature. Edged by high trees, wonderfully manicured lawns running to the terraced front, the high, stacked chimneys outlined against the sky, the whole place was breathtaking.

Ben did not look at Tara, and she was grateful. Her cheeks were quite red with annoyance and suspicion. He helped Miriam out and wheeled her forward, watching her face as she gazed at the manor.

'Twenty-one bedrooms, ten bathrooms, four reception, a library, a billiard-room and various other assets,' Ben remarked as Tara stood stiffly by to allow her mother to gaze even further.

'Why do you want such a huge place, Ben?' her mother asked. 'You're not even married!'

'And I don't plan to be, Miriam,' he assured her with a quiet laugh. 'In any case, I wanted this house more than anything else for business purposes.'

'Business? It's a beautiful house, a place to live in, to be cherished. You can't turn it into business premises.' Tara's outraged voice had him swinging to face her with sardonic amusement, his eyes flaring over her before he answered, his gaze bringing further colour to her face.

She was wearing a silky, pleated skirt, the matching top a loose camisole design that left her slender, tanned arms bare and showed off the graceful poise of her neck, and for a moment she felt quite vulnerable, out on a limb. She wished she had never spoken. Let him turn it into a factory for all she cared!

'My dear Miss Frost,' he said quietly, 'I do not intend to use the manor as a warehouse to store cartons of potato crisps. We're not in that kind of business. I live here. It's almost restored to its original state. I entertain a great deal, people from all over the world. Staying in my house, eating my food and walking in my garden makes them very mellow. Shall we say, it softens them up for the kill?'

There was no need to reply. A curvaceous brunette came out on to the terrace, linking her arm through Ben's, obviously deciding that she had been excluded enough. He had said that he was having a guest. He'd also said that he had women—plural. This one looked to be quite enough to be going on with.

'Ah, Wanda! Sorry to be so long, but I wanted to show Miriam and Tara around the lodge. You could order tea for us now.'

She did a great deal of clinging, Tara noted disapprovingly, and she didn't shoot off to obey orders either.

'Ben, darling, you drove back from the lodge. How lazy!' She had a voice like sugared melon, and Tara turned to shut the car doors, seeing no way of getting out of this tea-party. 'What a strange car!' Wanda carried on sweetly. 'Very functional. Part car, part ambulance.'

'And part battle-wagon!' Tara snapped, slamming the doors and turning to the fray.

Miriam had a dreadful attack of coughing that Tara ignored, knowing as she did that it covered bubbling laughter. Ben took over quickly, dislodging his clinging companion and wheeling Miriam forward.

'Wanda Pettigrew,' he said quietly, his eyes ignoring Tara. 'Wanda, this is Miriam, and Tara Frost. Miss Frost works for IST.'

'Oh, a secretary?' Wanda surmised.

'No, Public Relations,' corrected Ben, his eyes now on Tara with no particular favour. 'Her business is to charm people. Normally, she's very good at it.'

'Given the correct circumstances,' Tara said seriously, her eyes meeting his without flinching. She was glad, though, when he dropped any further social chatter and led them indoors.

'I imagine that a penny for your thoughts would be seriously undervaluing them,' he murmured as they entered the house and stepped into the hall. She ignored him and looked around, her annoyance lessening at the sheer beauty of the place.

She was prepared to hate everything, but she had to admit that it was a little like a conducted tour of heaven. Her dark, almond-shaped eyes widened with wonder as she followed the little procession. Ben wheeled her mother from room to room, pointing out the way it had been restored, introducing them to the staff who already had the manor in tight control. Wanda disappeared.

Tara's wonder began to die as she remembered the lodge and the preparations there, and she simmered with the need to speak out. Her chance came when later Ben suggested that her mother be served with tea while he conducted Tara around the upstairs of the house, and she knew that this was because he could hear her boiling. It suited her fine.

'Now that I've got you to myself, you can explode,' he said quietly as they climbed the lovely staircase, the sound of her mother talking gaily to the house-keeper making her realise why he was still being quiet His anger had grown, too. 'I've noticed that you've got something to say, but you're keeping it all inside until Miriam is safely out of the way.'

'I intend to,' said Tara sharply, her face flushed at the way he kept his eyes steadily on her. Her mind was fuming over the preparations, and her suspicions were sharp and dark.

'In here.' He opened a door and ushered her inside, and it was only as the door closed firmly behind them that she realised it was his bedroom.

'Yes. My room,' he said, with anger at the back of his deep voice, and her blushes deepened as she spun round to escape. 'Obviously you imagine that this is where you'll end up, so have a close look around. Anything you dislike I'll have changed.'

'Oh! I never thought . . .' He was so annoyed that it was quite frightening, and she reminded herself once again, belatedly, that this was her boss. He was blocking her way out, quite deliberately.

'You normally speak your mind,' he rasped. 'That's the first time that I've heard you lie, too. Here we are, Miss Frost, all alone. Let's have it,' he ended testily.

'All right!' Tara faced him and went in head on. 'It was only yesterday that I told you about my problem with Mirry and you said you had an idea. Today, twenty-four hours later, there's a lodge on your estate converted for an invalid. You're good, Mr Shapiro, but not that good!'

'So, your worst forebodings having been confirmed, you're about to tell me that you will not accept the lodge even for Miriam's sake?' he asked, narrow-eyed.

'You know damned well that I'll have to! You know I can't refuse Mirry anything now, and she loves it here, that's plain to see. But if you think . . .'

'I think,' he said caustically, 'that you are on the very edge of dismissal, Miss Frost. I do not chase twenty-four-year-old girls!'

It annoyed her more than ever. It made her feel on the edge of being a child.

'I'm almost twenty-five,' she snapped. 'And in any case . . .'

'You behave like a fifteen-year-old,' he grated. 'No man in his right mind would want the task of turning you into a woman!'

He walked to the window that looked over the grounds, his back tight and angry.

'The lodge was coverted ten years ago,' he assured her quietly and bitterly. 'It was converted for my wife.' He spun round and stared at her, no smiling irony now in the topaz eyes. 'Debra was not injured in an accident like your mother. She had a progressive and incurable disease that first paralysed her and then killed her.'

'Oh!' Tara's face was white, but he looked at her coldly.

'I wasn't wealthy then,' he said flatly. 'I was just beginning. The house was mine and the estate, but I didn't have enough money to restore it. I restored the lodge, not to its former glory, but to a place where a dying woman could move fairly freely. We lived there. The bedroom upstairs was mine. I've had it all redecorated, not for Miriam, but because I hated the damned place. If it helps Miriam, though, maybe I'll keep it after all, and not have it demolished as I intended.'

'I'm so sorry! Forgive me, please.' Tara felt close to tears. His face was taut, bitterness edging the mouth that usually quirked with amusement, and she realised for the hundredth time that she did not know him at all, that one never really knew anyone.

'Take the lodge for Miriam,' he said impatiently, 'and then maybe I will forgive you.' He turned to look at her steadily. 'But not for some considerable time, Tara.'

'I'm sorry. I understand now why you took care of us when Mirry was injured. It must have brought back a lot of unhappy memories. I'm sorry that I'm so suspicious, bad-tempered. I'll do whatever you want.'

'Hah!' His bark of cold laughter had her dark eyes looking at him worriedly. 'What you thought I wanted a little while ago was entirely different. What sticks in my throat is the fact that you thought I would sneak up on you. If I wanted you, you'd know about it. I do not want you.'

'I'm sorry.' Tara hung her head and jumped with shock when his hand curved round her chin, tilting her face up.

'Maybe it's worth it to clear the air,' he said softly, the tension leaving him. 'At least I've had the distinction of receiving at least six apologies in two days from a very fierce young lady.'

'Why—why don't you just fire me?' Tara muttered shakily.

'Monetary value over nuisance value,' he said sardonically, releasing her and stepping to the door, leading her out. 'I look at you and I see pound notes. It adds a rosy hue to your very irritating presence.'

Right at that moment he could have got away with saying anything. She was utterly devoid of all thought but remorse. She had never expected to feel sorry for Ben Shapiro, but she did now.

Downstairs, Miriam looked as if she had taken as much of Wanda Pettigrew as she could, and Tara hastily drank tea and then begged to be allowed to go, using the growing darkness as an excuse.

'So you would like to come here to live?' Ben asked her mother softly, and, as Miriam's eyes turned anxiously to her, Tara stood up with a brilliant smile.

'Yes, please. We would!'

He nodded slowly, the irony back in his golden eyes, and she was never so relieved as when she saw it.

During the week he powerhoused back into her life. He arranged for them to move, for the flat to be put up for sale and for the village nurse to be employed. Tara queried nothing. He came several nights to the flat to talk, but his words were for Miriam, one principal to another, and Tara was excluded for the most part, her function to serve cups of tea and to sit watching. She had to admit that most of the time she was watching Ben, her slanting eyes moving over his face, seeing harsh lines beneath the smile, lines she had never noticed before.

She had trouble too with Martin. He had now been back for over a week and she had not once been out with him. When she told him why, he was furious.

'Helping your mother, my foot!' he said rudely. 'He's after you!'

'Don't dare talk about him like that!' Tara flew into a rage and stormed at him, the words out before she could stop them, her face flushing brilliantly when she realised that the door of her office was open and Ben Shapiro had heard at least some of the angry exchange. He just looked at her steadily and walked on. Martin left in the other direction and an hour later she was in Ben's office, her knees shaking for the first time as she wondered what he would say.

'When you get home, pack your things,' he said testily. 'There's not a damned thing happening in Omari. Joan has you booked on the first flight out tomorrow. You've got the rest of the day to organise it, get in the picture and make a few decisions.'

'You already sent somebody out there,' Tara reminded him anxiously, no longer able to stand up to him as she had always done, her attitude softened now.

'Unwillingly and erroneously,' he snapped. 'He's coming in as you go out.' He suddenly looked up. 'This is no picnic, Tara. You stay in the capital and you work from there. Have you had the necessary jabs topped up recently?'

'I'm always up to date,' she told him quietly. She was. She never knew where he would send her next.

'OK,' he said softly. 'You stay in the capital, work from there, organise from there, report in from there. Do I make myself clear?'

Tara nodded and looked down, her face flushed again. Sometimes she meddled, and he knew it.

'What about Mirry?' she asked quietly.

'I'll move Miriam in,' he assured her. 'Leave her to me. No worries for you there. Just get out to Omari and do the job better than it's being done at the moment.'

'All right.'

Tara moved to the door, suddenly quite tearful. It would have been nice if he hadn't been so hard. It would have been nice if he had said goodbye, good luck. She supposed that she deserved this attitude, but with no warning it hurt her.

By Friday she was in Omari, and Ben Shapiro had taken over her commitments in England almost as of right, fitting her private problems into the vast organisation of his days, his restless energy swallowing up such trivia.

CHAPTER THREE

TARA brushed her hand tiredly over her eyes. It was so hot. There was not even a faint stirring of the sluggish air. Both the front and back of the hastily erected tent were open, but it made little difference when the temperature outside was over forty degrees centigrade. The flies were the present nightmare, swarming around the place, biting every unprotected surface of skin. Hell must be like this, she thought miserably.

Over two weeks and she was still here. She had long since ceased to worry about Ben's reaction when he had received her last report. She didn't need to have been there to know that there would have been an explosion, but her mother was fine, she had telephoned and made sure of that before taking on this extra work.

It was a far cry from the capital and the delights of the Grand Oasis Hotel but it was here that the help was needed, right here where the disaster had struck. The water was now gone. The dry earth soaked in millions of gallons, the searing sunshine took care of the rest. Now there were the injuries, the homeless and the dirt. This was not her job, but she had not been able to board a plane in her white linen suit, her skin bright and fresh, when out here the devastated people waited for help.

'You are able to carry on, Tara?'

The French doctor looked up from his task of giving injections, and Tara nodded gamely. Individuals were

always quick off the mark, what a pity that whole
countries couldn't act with the same speed. There were
people out there boiling in the sun, freezing at night
when the temperature fell dramatically; talk was cheap!

The IST trucks and supplies were already on their
way, that had been her first task as soon as she had
landed. One more day and they would have left
Kadina, been at sea on the wrong ship, difficult to re-
route. Ben had been right to send her out urgently.
The sturdy Land Rovers were needed here to ferry
things about in terrible conditions. As for herself, she
was a willing dogsbody, no nurse or doctor, but so
many people were needed and at least she could fetch
and carry, give comfort.

She broke into a new box of medical supplies, noting
with a sinking heart that the supplies were dwindling
fast, sweat from her forehead dripping on to the dull
brown cardboard.

'*Dieu merci!*' Dr Lepage's thankful words had her
lifting her head, and she felt a surge of pride in
achievement as the thunder of engines drowned any
other words, the smell of diesel oil like perfume to her
nostrils as the IST vehicles rolled noisily past. They
were here! A small help, but a very necessary one, and
they carried more supplies of medicine, she had seen to
that.

She lifted the heavy box and staggered to the table
with it as the engines were cut and the noise faded
away. One more minute and she would go out there to
greet them. She began to empty the box quickly, only
looking up when she realised that there was no sound
at all in the tent. Everyone had stopped talking, and she
saw why.

Ben Shapiro stood like a giant in the doorway, his powerful body in khaki shirt and shorts, his hands on his lean hips as he stared at her furiously. It was such a shock that for a moment she swayed dizzily, and Dr Lepage called out, but Ben was there first, his hand on her arm, his amber eyes blazing with anger.

'Well, that's one way to escape,' he grated, 'but believe me, when you come round, I'll be right here and still as mad as hell!'

'I—I'm not going to faint,' said Tara slowly, her world righting itself, her wide eyes looking up into the severe face with not much hope of getting out of this.

'What the blazes are you doing here?' he demanded, taking her arm more tightly and leading her to the back opening of the tent where he could shout at her in some little privacy.

'I had to come! There's so much to do—too much! The sheikh is here!'

'But not his sweet little daughter!' Ben rasped. 'Don't let his robes fool you, he's a man and tough as old boots.'

'I don't need sarcasm!' Tara managed tightly, but he spun her to face him with no sympathy for her opinions at all.

'What you *do* need I hesitate to deal out here, but it's right at the top of my mind! Why did you leave the capital? I gave orders and I expect them to be obeyed.'

'There was so much to do, so many things needed, I couldn't leave,' she appealed to him, although she could see by his hard face that such appeals were useless.

'We're a firm! We're not a bloody nation!' he thundered. 'What good do you think it is for you to

stand here trying to pretend that you're the whole Red
Cross?' He flicked at her arm as a fly rested there.
'You're too far gone to even notice when you're going
to be bitten.'

'If you'd left it, it would have drowned,' Tara said
dully, her hand wiping aimlessly at her wet face and
neck.

It was a mistake, it drew his attention to her skin, and
he muttered furiously, 'What are you doing for those
bites? You can get infected here with no trouble at all!'

'I'm seeing to them at night when I get back to my
hotel.'

She wanted to ask him why he was here, how he had
managed to come with the trucks, what he intended to
do, but he was not in a very receptive mood, to put it
mildly, and she decided to let it wait a while.

Ben, though, was not waiting.

'If you've got anything here that belongs to you, then
pick it up,' he snapped. 'You're leaving now and you're
not coming back! And don't say a word,' he added
furiously when she opened her mouth to protest. 'This
is not what I pay you to do. Disasters do not need
amateur do-gooders! You're going back!'

Any argument would be useless, she knew that, and
anyone who imagined that they could restrain Ben
Shapiro physically had to be mad. She went with him.
He would have dragged her anyway, she had little
doubt of it.

He used one of the Land Rovers, lifting her bodily in
and slamming the gears into place.

'It's late now,' he said quietly, his voice like steel.
'Tonight you stay at your hotel, tomorrow you go to
the capital and you're out of here on the first flight.'

'Back to the office?' Tara wailed, her eyes filled with reproof as they drove through the edge of the devastated township.

'The office? Miss Frost, you are fired!' he told her with grating sarcasm. He ignored her silence for the rest of the drive to the mean little town beyond the flooded area, and Tara was too tired even to cry, let alone protest. She had always known that she was getting away with murder when she defied Ben. This time she had gone too far.

The hotel was the only one, and to call it an hotel was stretching the imagination to its very limits. There were a lot of limits to the place, anyway. The service was slow, the air-conditioning was non-existent, the rooms were barely clean. Ben looked at the huge fan that turned in a desultory manner in the foyer, and he grunted irritably, the only sound he had made all the way. He watched Tara coldly as she collected her key, and then walked behind her up the one flight of stairs, his opinion of her room obvious as he raised his eyebrows and then stared at her forcefully.

'I'm going to get a shower,' Tara said, feeling that even this mild remark had to be defensive.

'Do that.' He paced about the room in an irritated manner. 'Meanwhile, I'll book myself in here. It's too late now to drive on to the capital.' He jabbed a finger in her direction like a weapon. 'Tomorrow, however. Early!'

Tara refrained from dropping a curtsy, but she was beginning to be very annoyed herself. She glared at him and grabbed her robe, walking into her bathroom and closing the door with a bang.

It was impossible to keep on feeling angry, though,

and she bit her lip in remorse as she realised she had
not even asked how Mirry was. It was because she was
so tired, bone-weary, so hot. She looked with distaste
at the scarred and pitted shower base. She supposed it
was clean, but anyone who had not been here for two
weeks would seriously doubt it.

Ben hammered on the door, and she let her hand
drop tiredly away from the taps.

'I'm ordering a drink. What do you want?' he asked
briskly, his rage apparently having subsided a little.

'Iced tea, please.'

'You look as if a double brandy would do more
good!' he rasped, and didn't seem too pleased when
she gave him a short, breathless lecture on the danger
of spirits in hot climates. 'Just shower! I'll think,' he
told her irascibly.

Tara turned on the water; even that was warm,
improving to tepid after a few seconds. It was wet
though, blessedly wet, and she stood under it
thankfully, wincing as it brought her bites to stinging
life. She turned, letting the water pour over her,
lowering her head to let the cool blast on to her nape.

Then everything inside her shrank with revulsion,
her stomach tightened and her mouth opened to
scream as she saw the gigantic spider crouching on the
inner edge of the shower. She leapt out, racing for the
bathroom door, certain that it pursued her, little sobs
of terror at the back of her throat as she burst into the
bedroom.

Afterwards she remembered that Ben hadn't looked
shocked at all. He simply sprang into action, shooting
to his feet and grabbing her, his face questioning.

'Spider!' she whispered through trembling lips, her

whole body shuddering, and he strode off into the bathroom to deal with it.

When he came back she was still shaking like a leaf in a storm, her arms crossed over her, only realising how she looked as he carefully shook out a towel and tossed it to her. He looked a bit disgusted, and she hastily wrapped the towel around her.

'I—I'm sorry. I know I shocked you.'

He glanced up, away from his task of shaking her robe vigorously.

'The spider shocked me!' he said tightly. 'God, I've never seen anything so big! As to the female form, one is pretty much like another, except that you're pint-sized. Get dried here!' he ordered gruffly. 'I'll turn my back.'

He put her robe where she could reach it and she hastily dried herself, ignoring the pain as she rubbed the sore places on her arms and legs and the top of her back.

'Thank you.' Secure in her robe, she tossed the towel down and Ben turned around, his eyes on her suddenly pale face and then on her arms.

'Where's that stuff for those bites?' he asked aggressively, and she pointed to the small jar of ointment that Dr Lepage had given her. She reached for it, but Ben removed it angrily from her fingers. He was just rubbing it carefully on her arms when the door opened after the briefest of taps and a waiter brought the iced tea.

He looked stunned, but then he always did, Tara mused as he shuffled in, his slippers dragging irritatingly, his mouth slightly open. Tara had wondered during the past two weeks if he was in fact a zombie. She wondered if he would make it across the room.

Ben's fingers stilled on her arm as he looked up, and then he blazed at the waiter in French. He even startled Tara, and she was used to him. The waiter came to astonished life and discharged his duties rapidly, and as he left Tara burst into hysterical tears, laughing, crying and shaking at one and the same time.

It took a minute to realise that she was tightly in Ben's arms, that the angry voice was quiet and soothing, and that he was rocking her against him gently. It was funny, she thought after a few seconds when her tears had stopped but he still went on holding her, she had been shuddering with revulsion, the tears only the aftermath of her fright in the shower. Now, though, she felt bemused, strange sensations flaring through her. She lifted her head and looked up at him, her body resting against his, tired, relaxed, and he looked down at her, his topaz eyes still filled with a faint anger.

'You are one hell of a handful!' he suddenly bit out.

'I can't seem to please you, so I don't try much,' she confessed softly, her mind not at all on this.

The questions she was asking herself were deep inside. Why did she feel like this? What was different? Maybe it was the shock, the tiredness. She realised that her hand had gone out to touch his face, almost experimentally, and dimly she felt his body tighten in surprise.

'It's because I'm tired, I expect,' she murmured sleepily, and he swung her up into his arms, sitting her on the bed, plumping the pillows behind her, his hands strong and capable as he served the iced tea and handed her a cup.

'I'll go and book myself into this place,' he said grimly, and simply walked out.

Tara drank the tea slowly, her eyes half closed, her body unwilling to come out of the strange lethargy. He had been berating her soundly since he had arrived, but not once had she felt anger. It was strangely comforting to have him here. It must be that thing about a face from home. She put her cup down and slid lower on the bed, closing her eyes completely.

The pain in her shoulders wakened her, the pain and the irritation. A spasm of protest crossed her face and her eyes opened reluctantly, widening in surprise to see Ben standing looking down at her.

'What's hurting you?' he asked in a tight voice before she could speak.

'My shoulders. It's nothing,' she said defensively, not wanting another outburst.

'Let me see.' He reached out for her, pulling her forward and upright, in spite of her protestations that there was nothing at all. She was turned, her legs swung over the edge of the bed, her back towards him before she could really wake up.

'My God!' His hands slid the robe from her shoulders, exposing the smooth skin that was now brightly scarred with bite marks.

'I couldn't reach there,' she confessed in a low voice, her head bent vulnerably. She felt incredibly guilty about it, as if she had done it on purpose to irritate him, and he left her for a second to get the ointment, saying nothing at all. It saddened her surprisingly to feel that he was even annoyed when she hurt so much.

The ointment was soothing, his hands cool and sure, and after a second she dared to relax, allowing herself to lean against him, her head still drooping.

'That's it!' he said briskly when the soothing movement of his fingers had lulled her back into that strange earlier feeling. She was lethargic again, almost dreaming, and his voice was edged with laughter as he spoke again.

'You haven't gone to sleep?'

'No.' She lifted her head. It felt so heavy, so did her eyelids, but she kept them open to allow her to look at him, her head turned to see his face. He seemed to be too still, his hand coming back to massage the back of her neck, his eyes running over her, and she blushed softly as she realised that her robe had parted slightly, that the rise of her breasts was visible.

'I—I don't really know what's the matter with me,' she whispered, hypnotised by his amber eyes.

'Reaction,' he said quietly, not moving away, not stopping the slow movements of his fingers.

'Ben?' She lifted her face as he moved away a little, and his eyes darkened to deep honey as he came back to her, his hand in her hair as his mouth covered hers unexpectedly.

It was so comfortable, so warm, so belonging. Tara made no move to free herself from this dreamy rapture. Instead, her eyes closed and her head came to his shoulder with a more than willing acceptance of this. Oddly enough, it was no shock to her. There was something so right about it. When Martin kissed her, as he often did, there was a hidden aggression that made her feel trapped, her feeling when he released her that she had just escaped something a little worrying.

There was no aggression in this kiss, and she had not the slightest feeling of insecurity. There was no wish in her to pull away, to escape. It was when her arm moved to encircle his neck that Ben broke the contact, lifting his head and looking at her with unreadable topaz eyes. She felt as if she had somehow done something wrong, and guilt flooded through her, spoiling the moment.

'I'm sorry. I—I'm not myself,' she said, her face flushed and embarrassed.

'Apparently, neither am I,' he said drily. 'I don't normally comfort the sick and weary.' He stood and moved to the door. 'If this place can cope with the unexpected, then I think you should have a meal here in your room tonight and then get to bed. We start early tomorrow for the capital. If I can get you a flight out tomorrow, then you'll be on it!'

'What about you?' Tara asked anxiously, her eyes puzzled for more than one reason.

Surely if a man kissed a woman he didn't then simply walk away and ignore the fact? Nobody had ever done that with her before. Of course, Ben Shapiro had said quite definitely that he did not want her, and he was probably a little sorry for her now. He was probably disgusted with himself, too. She felt wildly irritated with him, her gaze sharp and hard on his face.

'You are the one getting out of here!' he said determinedly. 'I'm staying for a few days. There are things to arrange now that the vehicles have arrived. I'll have to stay and do it. I imagine that the office can cope without me for a while.'

'It's my job to arrange things like that,' said Tara heatedly, all the languorous magic now gone.

'True enough,' he agreed, giving her a slightly withering look. 'But you're not in any condition to manage.'

'After a good night's sleep, I'll manage well enough,' Tara snapped, meeting his cynical gaze.

'We are not about to put that to the test,' he replied, his eyes punishingly on her. 'It may have slipped your mind, but you are fired, Miss Frost!'

He went out then and Tara stared blankly at the door. He meant it! It had not just been a momentary flare of annoyance. She was fired. All she had done was help people. What about the lodge? She hadn't even asked about the flat. One thing was sure, she would not sell now.

She rang for service. She had no wish to eat with him anyway, and for good measure she faced the terrors of the bathroom and washed her face, scrubbing away at her lips to make sure that nothing of Ben Shapiro remained.

Next day they arrived in the capital, walking into the luxury of the Grand Oasis Hotel by early afternoon. Even after a good sleep the night before, Tara had to admit that she was very tired, and the journey hadn't helped at all. She knew that she had been very silent, and Ben had left her to it. She didn't see at all why she should talk pleasantly to someone who had just fired her, and as he seemed to have dismissed her entirely from his mind, too, keeping silent had been no problem. In any case, she had slept most of the way, in spite of the rigours of a desert drive in a Land Rover.

The air-conditioning worked here, though. Everything worked, and she relaxed in her room as Ben went out to book her flight. He had pointedly booked them in for one night only, so she knew that not only was she going but that he was definitely staying. His room was next door, and she felt like throwing a shoe at it. She refrained from childish temper, however, and rang for tea. She also asked for a menu. There was no way that she would go down to dine with her ex-boss.

In point of fact, he did not invite her. He simply came in to say that her flight left at nine the next morning and that he would take her to the airport. After that he went about his own affairs and left her to hers. It was humiliating and irritating, as if she had been sent to her room, although she had not planned to leave it.

What did he imagine was going to happen about the lodge? There was no way that she would stay there and wave cheerfully to him as he came to visit Mirry. His days of visiting Mirry were over. Her mother would not take kindly to this high-handed dismissal, either. It was not the first time she had disobeyed orders, and more often than not the very fact that she had acted on her own initiative had brought goodwill and business their way that had astounded Ben Shapiro. He had admitted that more than once.

Tara was still angrily mulling over his many crimes as she got ready for bed. There was no spider in this bathroom and she lingered under the cool shower, emerging feeling cleaner then she had done for two weeks. The bites too felt less painful, and she twisted around before the long bathroom mirror to get a look at her shoulders. They needed more ointment, but they were as unreachable as ever and she certainly wasn't going to ask for assistance.

He was sitting in the only easy-chair in the room when she slipped into her robe and padded back to her bedroom.

'How did you get in here?' she demanded angrily as he stared at her with cold, accusing eyes.

'Quite easily,' he assured her severely. 'You failed to lock the door. Be thankful that I'm not a love-starved Arab waiter.'

'Mostly, they're French,' she got in smartly, but by the look on his face they were even worse.

'How can I help you?' Tara asked in her best Public Relations voice, and it did nothing to ease his temper at all.

'I've come to put the ointment on your back,' he snapped. 'Tomorrow night you'll be home and Miriam can do it. Or Martin,' he added derisively.

'Martin does not look at my back!' Tara exclaimed angrily. 'And I can manage by myself, thank you.'

'As you did before?' he asked scathingly. He stood and looked around, homing in on the jar before she could snatch it up. 'Let's get it over with. It's going to hurt you more than it hurts me!'

He looked at her coldly as she stood defiantly at bay.

'I intend to do this, Tara,' he told her forcefully. 'Those bites are very bad. They'd had no treatment at all until I looked at them last night. If you weren't given to childish actions, you would have asked that doctor to see to them.'

'He was too busy to bother with little things like

this,' Tara snapped, backing away as he advanced.
'He had really sick people to see to.'

'I doubt if he would have been too pleased when
you went down with blood poisoning,' rasped Ben. 'If
you don't stand still, I'll whip that robe off and we'll
be back where we were yesterday.'

That did the trick, for more reasons than one. In the
first place she still felt very shy about that particular
little scene, and in the second place it reminded her
how she had felt when he kissed her. She sat huffily
on the bed and slipped the robe about one inch from
her shoulders. He pulled it further down with an
insensitive gesture, as if he were dealing with a lump
of clay, and began to apply the ointment with a certain
angry vigour.

'It smells revolting,' Tara muttered, wincing with
pain, and his hand gentled at once, smoothing it
carefully into her skin with a light touch that was
increasingly blissful.

'Chanel haven't got around to producing this sort of
thing,' he murmured dismissively. 'Maybe next time.'

'There won't be a next time!' Tara said, pouncing
on his words quickly. 'Having been fired, I shall most
definitely not be going out to unheard-of places
again.'

'That's true,' he agreed pleasantly. His hand pulled
the robe further down, and she stiffened with fright.

'That's all,' she got out sharply. 'There are no more
bites.'

'Wrong!' His hand began smoothing in more
ointment. 'These are not so bad yet, but they're
decidedly present. I expect they got at you through
your shirt. You seem to wear very little.'

Suddenly, Tara's throat was dry, her heart racing like a train, and, when he declared the medical help finished and wiped his hands on a tissue, she still sat there feeling peculiarly vulnerable, her head bent.

'What's the matter?' he asked with a certain amount of irritation, pulling the robe back on to her shoulders. 'Did I hurt you?'

'No,' she whispered, a shiver running over her as his hand touched her skin. She was scared now, beginning to realise that he probably could hurt her in a way that he would never know. The surprise of it kept her silent. She had always fought him, after she had stopped relying on him. There was no way that she dared to face him feeling as she did at this moment.

He turned her. He took her shoulders and made her face him, but she refused to look up, he couldn't make her do that willingly. He did it by taking her chin in his hand and tilting her face to his.

'All right,' he said grimly, his eyes on her trembling lips. 'This is where we finish off the treatment, just like last time.' He kept his hand on her face and brought his mouth to hers swiftly and fiercely.

It was a kiss very different from last night's, she realised in fright. The exasperated force of it took her by storm, his lips parting hers impatiently, his tongue invading her mouth with no hesitation, and wild feelings hit her: piercing shafts of delight, a painful sexual awareness that she had never before felt with anyone.

He lifted his head, the topaz eyes clear and alert, reading her expression, feeling the way she yielded against him, her dark, tilted eyes drugged with new and melting emotion, and he jerked her back to him, his mouth hard and insistent, the kiss deepening until small, mindless sounds drifted from her lips.

His hands slid beneath the thin robe to caress her shoulders as his lips eased away, brushing hers now with light, tantalising movements that did nothing to calm her, and she searched for his mouth in frustration, her arms moving around his neck, her whole body begging him to stay, to continue.

'You,' he murmured tauntingly against the smooth skin of her neck, 'want me to make love to you. You want me to stay here or take you to my room. Do you know what you're doing? Do you know that your whole body is inviting me to be your lover? Is this why Lambourne spits fire when you can't keep a date? Is this why he's back there now walking about like a condemned man? Is this what he gets?'

'No!' She gasped with shock, her eyes accusing as she looked up at him. 'How can you think that of me?' She attempted to pull away, but he held her exactly where she was, staring down into her eyes, his face still and thoughtful.

'That's one hell of an admission from a miniature fireball,' he jeered softly. 'I don't for one minute imagine that you realise what you've just implied.'

She did though, belatedly, and this time when she pulled away he let her go.

'Obviously you think that I'm no—no better than I should be,' she whispered tremulously, her face flushed and unhappy, her eyes avoiding his.

'No,' he assured her coldly. 'I think you've been too busy being clever, learning your languages, your skills, tearing into every job you've been given. There's only so much that anyone can do in a day. You never got around to growing up, to realising that you're a woman.'

'Sex doesn't make anyone into a woman!' Tara said fiercely, her eyes angry now, the dreamy magic gone under the cool, derisive lash of his tongue.

'The knowledge of her sexual power does,' he asserted, his eyes noting her growing anger. 'You have never recognised yours. You fight it. When it hits you, you go overboard. Next time you might not be so lucky. Next time it may be a man who wants you badly, like Lambourne!'

'You certainly don't want me!' Tara blazed, shame filling her as she realised just what she had said. 'And I certainly don't want you!' she added wildly.

His eyes narrowed on her face, on the tight anguish of her body, her clenched hands.

'I like my women to be mature,' he said softly. 'I like them to know exactly what they're getting themselves into. I don't tell them that I love them, either, and that's the next thing you would want to know. As to your—afterthought, ask yourself why you always fight me, why you take to your heels whenever possible, why you avoid looking at me in the office. When you've answered that to your own satisfaction, you'll be a lot older and a lot wiser. And I still won't want you!'

He walked out and closed the door, and Tara stood like someone stunned. She could not think at all. She didn't want to take anything out to look at it. After tomorrow she was fired. She would have to make quite sure that she never saw him again. She had no idea how she had got herself into this situation.

CHAPTER FOUR

TARA was pale and quiet next morning as he took her to the airport. The place was exotic, she had noticed that on arrival, and it was crowded. There were tourists who had so obviously decided to get out fast, although the scene of the disaster was miles away. There were young people arriving, volunteers by the look of them. They were a whole lot younger than she was, and Tara's mouth tightened as she realised that she was being dispatched rapidly for the very same offence that they were about to commit—helping!

There was a young boy selling flowers to those who were leaving, his face rather wistful, and Tara turned her head away abruptly. It would be the last time that she would ever be in a place like this. The likelihood of another post with similar duties was remote. IST and Ben Shapiro were laws unto themselves. In Public Relations with any other firm she would be bored silly, attending meetings, racing around doing things that she would consider pointless. She sighed to herself, realising that she was as hard to please as he was.

She went to check her bags and then moved to the barrier as Ben rejoined her. One minute and she would be gone, her time with IST and this all-powerful, hurtful man over. She felt very much alone, although he was right next to her, towering over her, irritatingly strong-looking.

'When you get back, go straight home,' he said

firmly. 'You have four days' leave to recover from this.'

Tara spun round, her eyes astonished. He was even telling her what to do with her own time, and she had more than only four days coming.

'Four days' leave?' she flared. 'I'm fired.'

His eyes filled with cool amusement then, and he took her arm firmly.

'I've often meant to fire you,' he confessed, the smile growing, all the old irony back. 'I never seem to get around to it, though, because generally speaking you're so damned good at your job. I was angry, worried at the state you were in, irritated by your disobedience, plenty of other things, too. I really enjoyed telling you that you were fired. I actually said it several times and I'm inordinately proud of myself. I didn't mean it, though.'

Tara stared at him, open-mouthed, and then sheer fury grew inside her. He had caused her all this suffering!

'Then I quit!' she snapped violently, tears of frustration in her eyes at this easy cruelty, this overriding ability to dominate.

He brought his hand from behind his back, holding out one long-stemmed flower, exotic but delicate.

'Forgive,' he suggested, amused.

It was in her startled grasp before she could refuse it, and he smiled derisively into her flushed and angry face.

'I mean it!' she raged. 'I'm not coming back!'

'Nonsense,' he said firmly, and she turned and stormed off. Hateful, impossible, overbearing man!

Half-way across to the aircraft, it all sank in and she felt more puzzled, more angry than ever. She turned for one last furious look, and he was standing on the observation balcony, so noticeable among the other people. His hand came up, not in any friendly farewell, but with four fingers spread out clearly. Four days. He often used those long, expressive hands to signal orders. He knew what he could do. His days of ordering her about were over.

Even before she had boarded the flight, though, she knew that she would go back. After all, she loved her job, and then there was the lodge. Mirry liked Ben too; if she knew anything about all this she would be very upset. It would be better to go back. She would go on ignoring him as usual. She would totally forget what had happened. He had said that she was clever. She would show him just how clever she was.

She looked carefully to see if he was still there, but of course he wasn't. Typical. She had no idea what had happened when he had held her and kissed her, but she was going to put that right out of her mind, because this had shown her one thing most clearly—she really did dislike Ben Shapiro! Slowly but surely she was beginning to recognise that the danger that lurked in those golden, ironic eyes was very real. Martin could have dinner dates to his heart's content!

Three days later she was back to normal. It was beautiful weather and she had to admit that she was glad to be out of the frightening heat of Omari. She had simply lazed about in the garden, pottered about in the lodge and walked in Ben's woods with impunity, knowing that he was not even in the country.

Martin had been up twice to collect her and take her out, and she could leave Mirry with no qualms whatever. The nurse that Ben had recommended was a treasure, already her mother's close confidante and really good at her job. She was a gossip, too. Tara had found out things that she really didn't want to know. Nurse Lewis apparently had cared for Ben's wife in this very place. That was how he knew her.

'So very sad,' she said softly. 'Such a beautiful woman. There was a strained atmosphere, though, almost all the time. I could sense it. I expect it was hard for him being so full of life and her being more and more incapacitated. She seemed to resent him, although no man could have done more for a woman than he did for her. He hardly ever left the place. Working like mad he was, to get that business going, and straight back here at night to sit with her. They both knew, though, that it was only a matter of time.'

Tara could have done without that information, but it explained many things. It explained his attitude to women, for one thing. He was obviously still in love with his wife. All his energies went into the business, the women he knew just objects to pass the time. He was quite soulless, which was alarming. Her feeling of pity for him had long since fled, because he was a man who needed nothing of the sort, in fact he didn't need anything. He was utterly self-sufficient, toweringly alone. She wondered how he could bear it.

He rang on the morning of the fourth day, his voice brisk and determined.

'I'm back and I want you on the job tonight, Tara,' he said forcefully. 'There's a reception and I'm taking you. I'll pick you up at seven. I have to come back to change, so it will be easy to collect you and then come right on back in.'

'I'm still on leave,' Tara reminded him pertly. 'I begin tomorrow, and even then the company owes me two weeks and a bit. Take Joan!'

'I can't spare you, so stop whining!' he rasped. 'Patrick Ndele is going to be there tonight, and I want you right alongside me. Joan is excellent at her job, but this is out of her league. You turn Ndele's blood to syrup. Dress for the part and be ready when I call.'

'I'm Public Relations, not Personal Relations,' Tara fumed loudly. 'I wasn't hired to procure!'

'Watch that tongue,' he bit out. 'Remember that you've been fired once. It can all be done again.'

'I'll come,' Tara said angrily, 'but I won't charm. I'll be a dead weight all evening.'

'We can safely leave the charm to Ndele,' Ben grated. 'I found him a very hard-headed individual, but when he speaks of you he goes all dreamy-eyed. Don't worry, I won't let him cart you off to his harem!'

'He doesn't have one,' Tara blazed. 'He's a Christian gentleman.'

'What's that?' he enquired sarcastically. 'A rare species? Just be ready.' He slammed the phone down and Tara counted slowly to ten before walking out to Mirry.

'Was that Ben, dear?' her mother asked, taking a close look at her face.

'It was.'

'I thought so. You two always fight so loudly.'

Tara was speechless. What did she mean, 'you two'? He put on the charm for Mirry; she ought to see him as he really was. Tara went upstairs in a very disgruntled manner to look through her wardrobe for 'charm clothes'.

It was obvious when he picked her up that he was not
filled with amusement at the way she had spoken to
him. His own charm was all for Miriam, and he
greeted Tara in no humorous way when she came
downstairs. He was big boss tonight, she noticed, and
she kissed Miriam on the cheek, assuring her that she
would not be long. Ben looked at her quizzically, but
she really felt that was true. He had no idea what she
was wearing. Her light cloak covered her from neck to
hemline. He had a treat in store, or perhaps a shock.

Once in his car, some of her courage deserted her. He
was very silent, his strong hands capable on the wheel,
his eyes intent on the road, and she had the distinct
impression that if she had not been there he would
have let the Ferrari have its head and roar down the
road. Something was annoying him, and of course it
could only be her. The knowledge kept her silent, too.

When they entered the hotel where the reception was
being held she was beginning to quake a little; her
defiant idea now not seeming so good, after all, and
when she swung her cloak off to hand it to the
attendant she was sure of it. Ben's angry gasp was
audible to anyone standing near, and it was not anger
that brought a quick flush to her cheeks.

The dress was a white shift, an expensive and
provocative creation. It was held at one shoulder by a
glittering clasp, the other shoulder left bare, the
material clinging to her small, clearly defined breasts
and her rounded hips. It ended a few inches from the
floor, a long slit to the knee making movement
possible. She had bought it on an impulse a couple of
years ago and frankly had never had the nerve to wear
it. As her eyes met Ben's, she realised that she did not

have the nerve now, either.

He stood quite still, looking at her angrily, his golden eyes dark with what she could only think was wild rage.

'I've a good mind to take you straight back home,' he bit out, his eyes flaring over her from her bare shoulder to her slender leg that showed tantalisingly through the slit. 'You're supposed to charm people with your sweet tongue, not your sexual allure. We'll lose Ndele for sure, he'll have a seizure!'

'I'll put my cloak back on,' Tara said coldly, her face now very bright and embarrassed, but he grasped her arm and took her forward at such speed that she found herself almost running to keep pace with him.

She soon found that she was not to be let out of his sight. For most of the time his hand was hard and tight on her arm, as if he dared not let her go. No doubt he expected that left alone she would have done something quite disgraceful and tarnished the name of IST. It was quite ridiculous, she decided. There were plenty of ladies here who looked to be barely in their dresses at all. After a while she began to feel quite demure, although Ben's rage was still quietly boiling just below the surface.

He need not have worried about Patrick Ndele, either. He took no notice whatever of her dress and talked to her animatedly about the progress in Kadina, his five children, his opinion of the English climate and her latest project. He was a damned sight more sympathetic than Ben Shapiro had been about her trip to Omari too, and she wondered if after all she should apply for a job overseas, in Kadina, for example. Christian gentlemen of his calibre were sadly lacking in England. Only last night she had needed to be quite

firm with Martin, who thought that a kiss should go a
great deal further.

That thought brought Ben Shapiro and the Grand
Oasis Hotel back into her mind, and her cheeks flooded
with colour. Ben's eyes were on her as she looked up;
he seemed to be regarding her with a great deal of
distaste. It served him right! He should be a little more
human and a little less interfering. She found her eyes
following him as he talked with some of the beautiful
women there, and she wondered which one he would
arrange to meet at some later date. It suddenly
hardened her and she began to seriously discuss the
possibility of a job in Kadina, to Patrick Ndele's
delight. She did notice that his eyes too strayed to Ben
Shapiro, and there was a faint thread of anxiety in his
glance.

Her opinion of him as a Christian gentleman fell to
zero when later Ben came to speak to them and her
champion told all.

'She's under contract to IST,' Ben said coldly,
adding with a smile at her that contained hidden
malice, 'In any case, believe me, you wouldn't want
her. She flies into a rage for next to nothing. I only
keep her for her entertainment value. Within a week
she would have antagonised every member of your
cabinet. She also has commitments in England, her
mother is an invalid. I don't suppose she mentioned
that?'

To Tara's chagrin, Patrick Ndele looked greatly
relieved, called her a teasing little creature, kissed her
hand and left to join other guests.

'How dare you? How *dare* you?' she raved quietly as
Ben smiled down at her triumphantly.

'With the utmost ease and with a clear conscience,'

he said flatly. 'Business is business. You're an asset to my business. Letting you go would be like selling the family silver.'

'I can leave whenever I want, and if I get a better offer, I'll do just that!' she snapped. 'I'd like to work overseas, and next time, you'll not get the chance to stick your oar in.' She looked angrily round the room. 'There are plenty of people here who . . .'

'In that case, we'll leave now,' he said smoothly, leading her to the door. 'Our business here is over. You have done well. The Kadina research is ours, in spite of Wainwright's procrastination. I've talked to plenty of useful people and a few beautiful ones,' he added quietly, a smile touching his lips. 'All in all, I'm well satisfied.'

Tara kept silent on the way back to the lodge. It might have been a success for him, but for her the evening had been nothing of the sort. She had ranged in emotions from anger to fright to frustration, and here he was delivering her home like a wayward child who had only just managed not to disgrace herself.

He pulled up at the gates of the lodge, switching off the engine and bending to glance at the windows.

'It looks as if Miriam is in bed,' he remarked. 'I'll not come in.'

Who had asked him? Tara made a move to leave, slightly hampered by the long cloak, and his soft murmur of laughter made her a little frantic, her hand clutching at the door.

'You're not locked in,' he assured her drily. 'All you have to do is stay calm and the door will open easily.'

'I'm quite calm,' she retorted angrily, although there was that certain breathless feeling again. He seemed to be filling the car, much too close to her, and she still remembered his cutting words in Omari. It would be altogether a good thing to be able simply to leap out and run. One wrong move and he would accuse her of being provocative. 'I just want to get out of here fast and go.'

'Why? Don't you want to talk a while? Do I have to wait for a written report of your chat to Ndele?'

'There—there's nothing to tell you, really,' she said, turning to him in surprise at the reasonable tone he'd used. 'After all, it was only an exercise in Public Relations. He simply talked about himself, his country, his children. He asked me about Omari,' she added, a little worried, not really wanting that subject of conversation raised. 'He—he was sympathetic. He's going to help.'

'Do you think he will?' Ben asked quietly, his eyes piercing the darkness of the car, his intent look worrying her further.

'I imagine so. He's kept his word so far.'

'They need help faster than they're getting it,' he said sombrely. 'I've been drumming up help too, all evening.'

'Oh!' Tara looked at him in surprise, her dark eyes wide with pleasure. 'That was very nice of you. I—I didn't know.'

'That doesn't astonish me,' he said, giving her a wry look. 'What do you know, after all?'

Unexpectedly, tears flooded into her eyes and she turned away abruptly. It was no use trying to be nice to him. He was hateful, cold, derisive. He took her shoulders in strong, firm hands, turning her back.

'That was unforgivable of me,' he murmured.

'Everything you do, you do well. We're just on two different planes though, and God, you're irritating!'

He jerked her forward, pulling her against his chest, his hand leaving her shoulder to catch her head, his fingers spearing into her hair as his lips searched for hers almost angrily. It was not going to happen again! She wouldn't let it happen this time. She struggled furiously and he lifted his head, looking down at her seriously.

'There's no need to take fright,' he said quietly. 'I'm not Lambourne. I don't expect value for money after a nice night out.'

'I haven't had a nice night out,' she managed to snap, glaring into his eyes, although her whole body was trembling and she knew that he felt it.

'I made certain that you didn't,' he rasped. 'The dress was proof enough of what you intended. Wear that with Lambourne and you'll get trouble. It even provoked me.'

'I wore it to annoy you!' she gasped, shivering as his hand slid inside the warmth of her cloak, searching for her bare shoulder.

'You expect me to believe that?' he asked silkily. 'When you took that cloak off you were flushed like a rose. You looked like a cat ready to be stroked.'

'I was scared,' she muttered, shuddering as his hands explored the skin of her shoulder, his fingers running down her arm. He still thought that she wanted him to make love to her! She didn't know whether to scream or cry.

'You did well to be scared,' he murmured menacingly. 'I've told you that I pick my own women, they don't set out to captivate me, it's a real turn-off.'

'Then why are you touching me?' she asked
frantically, waves of feeling flooding over her. 'Why
don't you let me go?'

'Maybe you've succeeded where others have failed,'
he said in a low voice, his fingers unfastening the clasp
of her cloak.

Or maybe you're trying to teach me a lesson I don't
deserve, she thought wildly, pushing against his chest
in a futile gesture of panic. It was utterly useless, she
knew that as she did it, his lips were hot on the skin of
her neck and shoulder, and she felt a wave of
excitement shudder through her that almost drowned
the fear.

'I'll leave,' she gasped, her hands plucking uselessly
at him, knowing that she was going down in a tide of
feeling that she could not resist.

'You won't,' he breathed. 'You'll stay right where
you are, because if you leave you'll never see me again,
and you want me, don't you, Tara?'

Nothing in the whole world would have made her
admit that, although she suddenly and devastatingly
knew it was true. She wanted him to notice her, to want
her, to chase her as Martin chased her, to be eager for
her company, desperate to kiss her. In this case,
though, the positions were reversed. Ben suspected
every move she made. He praised her work and
damned her feelings. He confessed to needing her in
the firm, but watched her warily at all times, knowing
before she knew herself that she wanted to be right here
in his arms.

He gave her no chance to reply, either to admit or to
deny the truth of his assertion. His lips plundered her
mouth, his hands moulding her body in a way they had

never done in Omari, but then she had not provoked him in Omari. Even as she thought it, she knew that she had. She had been melting and willing, lingering against him. Tonight he had thought that the dress had been for him, to provoke him further, and it had succeeded.

'Please!' She tried to turn away but he captured her mouth again, his kisses devastating, allowing no escape. His hands brushed her breasts and then took possession as he felt them surge against his palms, a reaction she could not control. And did she want to control it? a voice inside asked weakly. Did she want to control anything?

The memory of last time blazed through her. Was she mad? She pulled violently away and he let her go with no demur, saying nothing. A silence stretched between them that seemed to fill the car, and Tara gathered her cloak around her with shaking hands.

'Don't ever touch me again,' she managed in a low, stricken voice. 'If you do I'll . . .'

'Don't make any threats, cat-eyes,' he said in a voice that showed he was not quite as calm as he would have had her believe. Never threaten something you can't carry out. Next time you provoke me, I'll touch you!'

She could tell that this was no idle threat. His daring far outweighed hers.

This time the door opened at her touch, making her suspect that before it had been locked from some central device, and she leapt out, running up the path into the lodge. He did not pull away until she was safely inside. Of course, he would not want to have to explain to Mirry how he had come to abandon her in the dark if anything had happened to her.

And something *had* happened to her, she admitted in the privacy of her bedroom. She had been locked in two strong arms again, mindlessly bewitched by fondling hands and determined lips. If she hadn't come to her senses, if he hadn't let her go . . .

In the mirror she looked different. She stood there in her nightie, turning her head this way and that. Twenty-four, and she had never felt like this before! She looked sultry, alluring. She felt alive! Maybe he was right. Maybe she had spent so much time being clever, that she had not been clever enough to become a woman. She lay for hours thinking about it, only falling into a fitful sleep when dawn came, knowing that in the morning she would look a wreck, admitting that this time it mattered. She wanted to look her best, wanted him to notice her, wanted to provoke him.

In the morning she had quite changed her mind. Uneasy sleep had robbed her of any lingering thrill, and the thought of facing Ben Shapiro was not at all daunting. She had done nothing wrong, his was the crime. She drove to work with a grim determination on her face, damning all men and one in particular.

Martin sauntered in early in the day, coming into her office as if he had every right. She had never noticed that before, but of course today was the first day of the rest of her life and her wits were sharp and keen.

'Sorry I didn't ring you last night,' he said quietly. 'I had a hell of a lot of paperwork, and it was after ten before I'd finished. I thought you might be in bed.'

'As a matter of fact, I was out with Ben,' she said with a great deal of satisfaction, secretly delighted with his reaction and striking herself a blow at Ben Shapiro even if he didn't know it.

'With Shapiro?' Martin was glaring instantly, and she couldn't help but notice that for a person who had never, according to Ben Shapiro, grown into a woman, she had a lot of men falling over her toes. 'Why were you out with him? What did he want?'

'My company at a reception,' she said pleasantly, going no further and leaving it hanging in the air.

The telephone rang and she picked it up with a regretful smile at Martin's furious face.

'Hello? Oh, put him on.' From the corner of her eye she saw Ben come into her office, but she studiously ignored both of them.

'Dr Lepage? Oh, Pierre, then!' She laughed softly, seeing Martin bristling beside her. 'Oh, I'm fine now. How are things going? Yes, I'd really love to! When you're in Paris next month? No, no. I'll fly out there to meet you. I have plenty of leave due.'

She burbled on and then put the telephone down with a self-satisfied smile, turning with feigned surprise to meet Ben's derisive smile.

'What did I tell you?' he remarked drily. 'You should have let him look at your back when you had the chance. He wouldn't have let the opportunity pass. The French are so susceptible to provocation.'

He waited until she glared, her face flushed and angry, and then he became big boss again. 'My office in ten minutes, Omari details wrapped up,' he said briefly and walked out.

'What's that about your back?' Martin demanded angrily as she sorted her files and gathered the notes she needed.

'I was bitten—by flies,' she added coolly as he seemed to be about to explode. 'Pierre was badly overworked, but as it happened, Ben came.'

'What about your back?' he repeated savagely.

'Oh, Ben rubbed some ointment into it. It was all right after that,' she said offhandedly.

Inside she was simmering, not only at Martin and his attitude, the way he seemed to imagine that she was some private possession, but at Ben and his snide remarks. She barely glanced up as Martin stormed out, and later, as she went to Ben's office, her temper and her nerves were vying with each other for supremacy.

The nerves won, but she need not have bothered. Apparently, to him, last night had not happened. It left her with the sneaking feeling that she was perhaps being childish. Maybe that was how people behaved. Well, she wasn't people of that description. She conducted the business with him in a cool, professional manner, the facts at her fingertips, irritated by the flare of pleasure that she felt when he said at the end, 'That's first-rate, Tara. The firm could use about ten more of your calibre. I suppose it comes from being a workaholic.' He spoiled everything by adding that. And not in any way a woman, she finished for him silently. She left feeling greatly subdued, grateful when Martin forgave her, even though she had done nothing wrong, except tease a little. She refused to go out, though. It was time that she stayed at home with Mirry and gained a little sanity.

CHAPTER FIVE

THINGS returned to an uneasy normality. At least, that was how Tara felt. Ben of course felt nothing at all, and that was quite obvious. His days were filled as before with driving energy, brilliant organisation and endless hours away from the office dealing with overseas commitments. The word 'overseas' seemed to have become a nasty word as far as Tara was concerned. If anything had come up that required her attention, then Ben certainly wasn't saying so. Not that she wasn't busy, there was enough work to keep her there late on many nights, and her excursions with Martin were few.

It seemed that Wanda Pettigrew was still very much in the picture, too. Tara walked into Joan's office one morning to hear her on the telephone, ordering flowers for Miss Pettigrew on Ben's account. She got out of there fast, hoping that her feelings were not showing on her face. For the first time in her life, the ugliness of jealousy was biting into her, making her feel almost ill, and it was ridiculous. She didn't want to feel a thing for Ben Shapiro. She kept Martin at arm's length even though she went out with him. Her job was all-consuming, a delight to her!

She felt even worse later that same week. She had gone with a query to Joan, something that needed one of Ben's personal files, but it was not there. Joan was snowed under with work, her manner unusually

77

offhand.

'It's in his office, Tara,' she said without looking up. 'Can you get it, please? It's on his desk. Go in, I don't think he's there.'

Tara tapped briefly on the door, however, just in case, but no reply being forthcoming she walked in. He was in there and so was Wanda. She was wrapped in his arms, lost in a deep kiss, and as Tara's face grew pale Ben raised his head and looked at her in surprise. She fled.

Ten minutes later he walked into her office, the file in his hand.

'According to Joan, you need this,' he said quietly, tossing it on to her desk. 'Let me have it back when you've finished with it.'

She couldn't speak to him. She couldn't even look up.

'Avoiding my eyes again?' he asked softly, the derision in his voice hurting and infuriating her.

'Naturally, I'm embarrassed,' she snapped, looking determinedly at the file.

'You could have knocked,' he suggested. 'It's usual.'

'I *did* knock! Obviously you were too busy to hear me!'

'Obviously,' he agreed. The strong brown hand came out, tilting her face, making her meet his eyes. 'Jealous?' he asked with a derisive smile.

'Why on earth should I be?' Tara said loudly. He shrugged, walking to the door, and then stopping to look at her for a long minute.

'You tell me,' he suggested softly.

When she took the file back, she handed it firmly to Joan, and when later Martin came in to make arrangements for the evening she responded wholeheartedly when he kissed her, hoping fervently that Ben Shapiro would just happen to pass by. He didn't.

The next day a memo came round to all staff. They were invited to a midsummer party at Ellerdale Manor; some overseas visitors would be there. Pleasure and 'business', warned a terse line in Ben's distinctive hand at the bottom of the sheet. It was an order and there was no getting out of it. Tara felt quite stricken. She was not at all sure how she would cope with this now. She had avoided any contact with Ben for days, and an evening where she would see him all the time was going to be little short of a nightmare. She would hang on to Martin and not let go. Guilt flooded through her at that. She was leading him on and it was wrong. It was Ben she wanted to hang on to, she admitted to herself, a hopeless wish.

When the evening of the party came, Tara had to face the fact that she actually did want to go because she wanted to see Ben no matter what it meant to her. In many ways, though, she was dreading it; dreading facing Ben, dreading finding out that his attachment to Wanda was permanent. She had stopped looking for a reason to hate him and had admitted to herself that she had been enslaved one way or another for a long time. She had fallen under the spell of the golden eyes, that sardonic half-smile. That this was all pointless, impossible, did nothing to alter the fact. She would go anywhere to see him, but do anything to keep him from finding out.

This was in many ways a great trial and Tara had decided as soon as she realised that this party was inevitable just exactly the dress to wear. She had a dress that had in fact never been worn. It had been meant for a party that she had been invited to on the very next day after her father had been killed, and in many ways it brought back sadness. She took it out of the wardrobe and its covers with mixed feelings. To allow it to colour her evening would be ridiculous, but it was black and it was a reminder.

She hesitated, uncertain about everything, but it complemented her pale hair, her slender figure, the newly acquired gold of her skin, and she set her lips firmly. This was important! She was going to show Ben that he meant nothing to her, and she would not allow a perfectly good dress to sit there in her wardrobe as a reminder of things that were now gone for ever. Nobody would wish it of her, least of all her father.

Dressed, she looked beautiful, although she did not see that. She knew, though, that she looked different. She had lost weight in Omari and not put it back on, and her eyes seemed to fill her face, tilted and wide, faintly shimmering. Her hair looked paler than ever against the black of the dress, and she suddenly saw the youthful look that Ben seemed to see, the lack of maturity. It was only a look. Inside she felt very aged, and he was quick enough to pile work on her, however immature he felt her to be. It gave her a spurt of anger at the downright unfairness of the man.

She went downstairs slowly, the chiffon whispering against the satin underskirt, the tiny straps that held the dress in place lying slight and delicate against her silken shoudlers, and Miriam stared at her for one long moment, her face softened, tears glittering in her eyes.

'So beautiful and so unusual, though I say it myself,' she said softly. 'Wear my pearls, Tara, they're just what that little dress needs.'

It was a relief to nod and turn away, a relief to them both because they had both been thinking of the same man at that time, and Miriam watched her walk lightly and gracefully into the other room, so slight and beautiful, so full of courage, so fair, like her father. She bit her trembling lips, sighing with gladness when Martin's car arrived, Nurse Lewis just behind him.

'Here's your escort and my babysitter!' she called to Tara, and for one small beat of time Tara heard unhappiness in that happy voice, knew that her mother felt trapped by her condition. She kissed her quickly and left, but the incident clouded her eyes and she had little to say to Martin on the short drive to the manor. Here she was, her mind filled with her hopeless desire for Ben, and her mother was denied all the things that people took for granted. It made her feel ashamed.

The manor was glittering with lights, although the day had not yet quite faded, and there were more expensive cars parked on the great circular drive that fronted the house than Tara had ever before seen in her life. She was glad of Martin's hand on her arm as he escorted her into the brilliant lights inside the manor, her heart thumping uncomfortably as she saw Ben almost at once.

'Good! You got here, I see.' He didn't seem too pleased about it, and Tara was suddenly filled with acute shyness that was edged with dismay as she took in the fact that Wanda was there, her hand clinging to

Ben's arm. His hostess, no doubt. From the way she looked, there would be no doubt in the minds of the other guests exactly what she was besides that.

'Drinks in the next room,' Ben said coldly to Martin. 'Get Tara a drink before she falls down. I'll hold her upright until you get back. Go with Martin, Wanda, will you, and see that he finds his way?'

They both left reluctantly, for different reasons, and Tara would have much preferred to follow them. She did not get the opportunity; when Ben Shapiro gave orders, everyone jumped. Wanda put on a sweet smile and Martin a very tense one, but they went and Tara watched them wistfully.

The usual firm hand captured her arm, and Ben swung her to face him, gazing intently at her for a moment.

'You're all eyes,' he said suspiciously. 'Beauty, fragility and mystery all captured in one girl. Fear not, he'll be back smartly, he only went with reluctance.'

'I didn't need a drink, either,' Tara said quickly, failing to meet his watching eyes, 'so he went for nothing.'

'At least it got rid of them both for a second,' he remarked tautly. 'Don't go on looking too brittle to touch. You're here to circulate, chatter sweetly in your fashion, and then, later, I need to speak to you seriously.'

She looked up in surprise, to be instantly captured by the amber blaze of his eyes.

'Why?' she asked, her eyes wide and puzzled.

'Don't jump the gun,' he warned. 'And keep it to yourself. It's private.'

He looked down at her steadily, his eyes skimming

over her, lingering on her shoulders. 'Tonight we're demure, are we?' he asked sardonically. 'I wondered just exactly what you'd come up with this time. Not the *femme fatale*, I see. A sweet little thing in a sweet little black dress. I bet Lambourne cuddled you as soon as he saw you. Keep him at arm's length tonight. I want everyone else to get a chance.'

'Oh, thank you!' Tara murmured bitterly, tearing her eyes away. 'Just what do you think I am? What function do you imagine I fulfil best?'

'That's a question that no girl asks,' he bit out, suddenly annoyed, sardonic no longer. 'Move out of my sight, though, and I'll chain you to my wrist. I need you to make a very good impression tonight for the firm, so watch your step. I'll be watching it too.'

'That's totally unfair,' Tara protested angrily. 'I can't count the number of times you've congratulated me on my tact and wisdom, and believe me, we all know that tonight is business only. None of us are fooling ourselves that we're invited to the manor as honoured guests.'

'What sharp claws you have, pussycat,' he murmured, his voice softening suddenly. 'You've been here as a guest before and you'll be here as a guest again. I feel quite certain that you'll cope normally, but this evening you seem to have got yourself a handicap. In any case, tonight you're slightly different. I don't know why, so I'm taking no chances. Here's your handicap,' he added scathingly as Martin returned, he and Wanda looking as if they had been running.

'And yours,' Tara said bitterly, bringing his eyes down to her with a swift, all-encompassing look.

'I'll take care of Wanda,' he said briefly. 'You just see that you come to me when I signal you, and control Lambourne. If he's making you look so weak and fragile. I wish I'd left him out of the invitations.'

He left abruptly, no doubt because Wanda's face was stiff with annoyance, and Tara tried hard to smile at Martin. She knew why she was different. She had finally given in to her feelings about Ben. She was wallowing in them and feeling very ill done by. If he was so clever, then why didn't he know that, too?

A small band struck up some dance music. The party was under way and she had her answer—Wanda was here, fully in possession. Ben's attitude to her made that plain. He didn't have time to notice anything else, and everybody from IST was supposed to be here to work. Do as I say, not as I do! When Martin held out his arms, a wide smile on his face, she smiled back brilliantly and moved into them. To hell with Ben Shapiro!

'I think I'll feed you,' Martin said, half-way through the evening. 'Your mind has wandered away again. I've been speaking to you for at least ten minutes and you've given all the wrong answers, mostly just little murmurs of sound that might mean anything. It's bad enough having to share you with half the guests as you do your stuff, without you working on in your head when you're rid of them!'

'Oh, Martin, I'm sorry! Maybe I'm tired,' said Tara, really embarrassed and contrite. He was nice. She had always been fond of him, ever since he had joined IST. He surely didn't deserve to spend his evening with someone whose eyes were constantly and reluctantly drawn to another man.

'Never mind,' he laughed, his little burst of frustration fading. 'It's probably low blood sugar. There's a splendid buffet in the next room. I'll fill you with protein, that should do the trick.'

'I'll try and eat,' Tara smiled, not at all sure that she could.

'It's either that or an injection,' he said with an evil leer at her that had her laughing at once.

Ben came into the room almost immediately; she began to think he had meant what he said about keeping his eye on her, and she hated the way her hands shook when she heard him close behind her.

'Let's sit down with this,' he said easily, deftly removing the plate from her grasp as if she were there with him and not with Martin, leading the way to a settee at the side of the room. 'Buffets are fine and cause little disturbance to the staff, but I can't handle a knife and fork while balancing my plate. It may be elegant to stand around nibbling things, but hunger gets to me swiftly on these occasions.'

'I think Tara needs a rest!' Martin said with annoyance in his voice that also clearly said, a rest from you! Ben swept one of his intent glances over her.

'We'll feed her up,' he said quietly, 'then I think I'll dance with her a while, if you don't mind. It's time that duties were over, I agree. Maybe you could take care of Miss Pettigrew of me, Lambourne? She'll begin to feel neglected.'

'Another duty?' Martin asked with a rasp to his voice that Ben ignored.

'The world is a sad and unfair place,' observed Ben

with a keen, slanting glance at Tara's trembling hands. 'Leave that here, Tara.' He removed her plate and placed it on a side-table as he swept her to her feet. 'With a bit of luck, someone will have eaten it by the time we get back here. Certainly you're not about to do justice to our extravagant cooking. What's the point of a French chef, I ask myself?'

He was talking simply to get her away from Martin, she knew that, and she imagined that now was the time for the private talk. It scared her into joining in the aimless chatter in an almost light-headed way as he guided her to the next room and swung her into his arms, moving smoothly to the music, taking her along with him.

'Do you have a French chef? How splendid you are!'

'Stop trembling,' he ordered, pulling her close, his hand warm at her waist. 'I'll never permit him to pounce on you and question you in rapid French.' He held her hand firmly, placing it against his chest and keeping it there, his thumb gently massaging her slender fingers. 'You're quite alarming tonight. Great big, dark eyes, long slender legs. If anyone so much as glances at you sharply, you'll probably burst into tears. What's the matter with you?'

'Nothing. I was actually enjoying Martin's company. We're both too busy to see much of each other at the moment. This invitation was a blessing.'

'Really?' he asked sarcastically.

He tilted her chin with one strong hand, his eyes holding hers, and she tried to move her hand, but he held it where it was, above the steady beat of is heart.

'Wanda isn't going to like this,' she blurted out,

panic-stricken about how she felt, wondering why he was doing this, what the talk was to be about. 'She's watching now. It's like being in a laser beam!'

'You can forget Wanda,' he grated. 'Leave her to me.'

'Gladly!' she snapped, her face pale at all she felt.

'What's happened to you?' he asked suddenly, his voice softer. 'Tonight you're different.'

'Maybe I'm tired, maybe I finally got bored with my job,' said Tara vaguely, her eyes roaming round the room, anywhere to escape that topaz gaze. He always saw too much, asked the most awkward questions. 'Are we supposed to be having that private talk now?' she added, glancing up at him.

'Later,' he assured her, his eyes running over her again. 'For the moment, I'm enjoying this.'

'Baiting me, you mean? I can imagine!'

'We're dancing,' he murmured in amusement. 'What do you want me to say? You dance divinely? You look almost unreal? I've changed my mind and I want you?'

Suiting actions to words he pulled her closer, his legs against hers, his hands coming around her waist to urge her against him. For a second she relaxed, taken by surprise, and his hands slid to her narrow hips.

'I think I've changed my mind,' he said, his face against her hair. 'Maybe it's because you're so tiny, like a small, clever, fastidious cat.'

His tongue touched the sensitive place behind her ear and she shot away from him rapidly, her eyes furious and hurt at this baiting. She would have walked off the floor but he held her too tightly.

'Pussycat, underfed cat and now—scalded cat!' he laughed.

'I believe I did warn you that Wanda was watching!' Tara said tightly, controlling her trembling with difficulty.

'But there's nothing for her to worry about, is there?' he asked silkily. 'She knows just where she stands with me. So do you.'

'I would now like to stop dancing,' Tara said in a small, hostile voice.

'Then we may as well have our private chat. This way.' He took her hand and set off at a fine pace towards the door, almost dragging her along with him, and she could not fail to see the eyes that followed their progress. Martin even took two steps forward, but nobody dared question Ben in this mood, not even Wanda.

'What will people think?' Tara gasped as he pushed her into a quiet room that was obviously the library, switching on the lights and facing her as he closed the door.

'The worst, no doubt,' he said. 'I have too much to do normally to bother about what people think, and right now we have some serious talking to get done before this evening ends. Sit down.'

There was nothing seductive about him now and Tara sat as ordered, taking a drink with no fuss when he simply decided what she would have and handed it to her. If he thought she needed one, then she probably did. She waited with trepidation for the speech.

'There's a possibility of an operation for Miriam,' he said without preamble. 'We're not at all sure yet, she would have to go to London for tests, but if it succeeded, she would be able to walk again.'

For a second Tara stared at him unbelievingly, and then her face lit up.

'I was told that she'd never walk again,' she gasped, excitement racing through her.

'Don't get over-confident,' Ben warned quickly, seeing her face. 'I said—a possibility, not a certainty.' He looked at her long and hard. 'There's always a risk in these things, but this man is a first-class surgeon, somebody that I trust. Miriam has to decide. So do you.'

'It's for Mirry to decide,' Tara said quietly, her face white. 'How—how big a risk?'

'Slight, but there,' he said firmly. 'There's always a risk. Maybe they didn't want to take it when she was newly paralysed. She's pretty strong now, healthy, thanks to you.'

Tara realised that she was in a stunned state of mind. Whatever she had expected, it had not been this. To have her mother walking again! How would it feel? Then there was the lodge to think of. Maybe her mother would want to go back to the city once she was well. A thought occurred to her.

'When did you find all this out?'

'While you were in Omari. I talked it over with Miriam.'

'And she never told me?' Tara asked with a stricken look on her face.

'I asked her not to,' he said impatiently. 'I wanted to tell you myself because I know the things you're going to say and I wanted to spare Miriam. The operation would have to be done privately, this man is worked

off his feet and there is a waiting-list for beds. So, the
choice is to have it done privately, or not have it for
months on end. I want to pay for it!'

'No!' Tara jumped up and he looked at her wearily.

'This is why I wanted to tell you myself,' he said
irascibly. 'I knew what you'd say. It has to be thrashed
out before Miriam comes into this sort of discussion.'

'She'll never agree to let you pay,' Tara said
fiercely. 'We already have the lodge, so many things
that you've done for us!'

'For Miriam,' he corrected tightly, 'and you know
why.'

She did; his wife, Debra, whom he still loved. She
felt almost sorry for Wanda.

'I'll pay! Somehow I'll manage it,' she said
determinedly.

'Oh, for God's sake have some sense, Tara,' he
rasped. 'Money means nothing to me. I can pay for
this and never feel it.'

'We would,' she said, her hands clenched at her
sides. 'We would feel it badly. Mirry is proud.
Already she has to have other people doing things for
her. She wouldn't . . .'

'All right,' he said in a suddenly softened voice.
'Mutual aid, then. You help me and I pay you; I
advance the money for the operation if it's to go
ahead, and you repay me later.'

It sounded too complicated to work out and Tara
stared at him a little anxiously.

'What exactly do you mean? How can I possibly
help you?'

'I need a hostess,' he said quietly. 'This place needs
a hostess, a central figure to give the place some

warmth.'

'So what's wrong with Wanda?' Tara asked heatedly, hardly able to believe her ears.

'Some people are good for one thing, some are good for another,' he said coolly. 'I want you for the hostess. It would simply be an extra job, to earn extra money. Weekends mostly, when I have guests, the odd evening. If it ran too late you could stay here overnight. There are plenty of spare rooms. You can have one permanently allocated to you and . . .'

'Like hell I will!' Tara flared, jumping to her feet. 'I can make money more easily and less painfully! If you think I'll jump at the chance to follow you around and sigh over you, then think again, Mr Shapiro! You're the only one with odd ideas, I wouldn't touch you with a barge-pole!'

He was on his feet too, against her before she could move, and he jerked her against the hard length of his body, his hands cupping her face cruelly, making her close her eyes in a panic, waiting for the pain that would surely come, knowing he was going to kiss her angrily. Even so, she was powerless to resist him, utterly unable to fight once he had his hands on her.

It did not happen.

'Are you going to stand there and let me punish you?' he asked drily. 'Any other girl with even half your spirit would be kicking and screaming. How fortunate that Lambourne can't see your face now.'

She opened her eyes and he was looking down at her with a derisive smile in his golden glance, his hands hard as he continued to hold her face up to his.

'I absolutely refuse to kiss you unless you beg, after that small but violent tirade,' he taunted softly. 'I know you've been waiting all evening for this, but honestly, kitten, I couldn't leave the guests!'

'You're absolutely hateful!' she said tearfully. She *had* been waiting all evening for this, without even realising it, but she was not about to confirm his suspicions. For a second their eyes held, and then she closed her dark eyes to shut out the gleaming magnetism of his, her body swaying softly towards him.

'Are you fainting or wanting to be kissed?' he enquired ironically, catching her and drawing her completely into his arms.

'Oh, please, Ben,' she whispered fretfully, hurt by the constant baiting. He cradled her head against his shoulder, his hand stroking down her face.

'Anything, when you beg so nicely,' he said quietly as his lips closed over hers. It was a bewildering shock. It happened every time to her and it frightened her as he tightened his arms around her, almost lifting her off her feet, his lips searching her mouth deeply, silencing the small sounds of distress that she uttered.

'It's all right, Tara! It's all right!' he muttered, his lips roaming over her silken shoulders, his fingers pushing aside the tiny straps to allow his hands freedom to move over her. 'Oh, God! I wish this party a million miles away and everyone with it!'

He searched for her lips again, devouring her hungrily in a way he had never done before, and she felt everything slipping away from her. It was impossible to think, to reason when Ben held her. He was kissing her as if he meant it, and she knew it was all a cruel joke. It would always be like that. She gave a peculiar little keening cry, trying to pull away, but

he held her fast and she suddenly knew that he was
not so entirely indifferent to her as he would have her
believe. Maybe he had talked himself into this feeling
with his constant attacks on her? Maybe Wanda was
beginning to bore him?

'Enough!' he said, pulling her head to his shoulder,
his arms tightly around her. 'This is neither the time
nor the place, and you look too fragile tonight. We'll
take this up at some later time, my strange little cat!'

For a minute he held her, his hands almost
soothing. For a minute too long. Without a knock,
without warning, the door swung open and Tara
opened dazed eyes to see Martin framed in the
doorway, his face livid.

'Tara!' He said her name at the top of his voice and
Tara knew that but for the music it would have been
heard by everyone. 'What are you doing in here?'

'I would have thought that it was quite clear to
anyone with normal vision,' said Ben witheringly,
anger stiffening his whole body.

Tara belatedly tried to draw away, but Ben held her
fast, his arm tightly around her, his eyes narrowed
and cold.

'So, you're playing around with the boss?' Martin
snarled nastily. 'I suspected as much!'

'Oh, we're not playing,' Ben rapped out sharply.
'It's all quite serious.'

'Serious? I know how you operate, Shapiro!'

'Not well enough, I think,' said Ben quietly,
releasing Tara. 'Stay here one moment longer and
you're looking for another job. At the moment you're
here as part guest, part employee, but whichever hat
you're wearing, this is my house and this room is

private.' His eyes lanced across to Tara's white face.
'Wait for me!' he ordered. 'I want a word with you,
Lambourne.'

He strode purposefully across the room and took
Martin's arm, forcing him out of the door and closing
it behind him as Tara sank to the nearest chair, her
colour returning in a rush, only to leave her again as
she realised just what had happened, what might have
happened in any other circumstances.

Escape was the only thing possible. When he had
finished dressing Martin down he would be back for
her, she had no doubt whatever about that, and before
then she had to leave. What she would say to Martin
she did not know, but she knew that her days of going
anywhere with him were over. It was her own fault,
and her fault too if he was now fired. She would have
to leave IST. She would have to get the information
that Ben had given Mirry, and then she would see this
surgeon and arrange it herself.

It took a great deal of courage to go back into the
lighted room, to behave as if nothing had happened,
but to her considerable relief nobody seemed to be
paying any attention to her return except Wanda.
Everyone else was talking, dancing, eating as if
nothing had happened.

She got her coat and went out through the main
entrance, just in time to see the tail-lights of Martin's
car disappearing down the drive, and she was not at
all surprised that he had left her. She would probably
have done the same thing in his place. She set off in
the darkness to walk to the lodge.

Ben's car came roaring down after her when she had
gone only a few yards, and he was out and standing in

front of her before she could run.

'Get in, you stupid little fool!' he grated. 'The way Lambourne feels at this moment, he's likely to be waiting to murder you!'

'Especially as you fired him,' Tara shouted, well enough away from the house to really give vent to her feelings. 'What do you imagine he thinks of me? It doesn't matter to you one tiny bit that my reputation is now mud! Did you hear what he said?'

'I heard!' he snapped, grasping her arm tightly. 'For your information I haven't fired him yet. It was quite obvious that to be able to get any sense out of him I would have had to knock him down and stand on him. I'll deal with Lambourne tomorrow. Right now, I'm dealing with you.'

'As of this moment, I quit!' Tara stormed, her hands clenched in fury, her eyes blazing in the dim light.

'The hell you do!' he told her tautly, forcing her into the car with no further ado. 'I'm taking you home. You've had more than enough for one evening. You can take tomorrow off, that way you don't have to face Lambourne.'

'Why should I not face Martin?' she jeered. 'He's only a man. You make me sick and I face you.'

She jumped nervously as he turned on her, his face savage.

'Yes,' he threatened, 'I'll make you jump, you thimble-sized virago! You and I have some unfinished business. You will now go home to the lodge. You will talk to Miriam with no thought for yourself but with only her needs in mind. You will come to a decision together. Tomorrow you will inform me. If

Miriam wishes to go ahead, I shall pay. Don't forget that you merely flutter irritatingly around the very edge of this affair. It is Miriam who needs the operation, and your feelings about me will not be allowed to get in the way.'

He brought the Ferrari to a halt at her gate with a force that threw the gravel up and threw Tara forward almost in a heap.

'My only feeling about you is one of utter loathing!' she started bitterly, swinging round on him.

He gathered her up as if she were a feather, crushing her against him, his mouth invading her furiously opened lips, and there was nothing seductive about him now. It was male oppression, male domination, his hands on her almost an insult as they slid roughly inside her coat, pulling away the fragile top of her dress to take almost brutal possession of her breasts.

She fought desperately, but the blood was drumming in her ears and he began to feather hot kisses from her jaw to her ears as he felt the surge of her breasts in his hard hands.

'Stop! Please stop!' she gasped, unwilling excitement racing through her blood.

'No!' he muttered furiously. 'Why should I stop? I stopped in Omari! Right now I ask myself if I was raving mad. You're delightful to touch and instantly willing. Maybe Lambourne has given you more experience than I thought. He didn't like to see his possession in my arms, did he?'

It was too much, her head fell back in defeat, acknowledging his domination and her own weakness.

'I'm not his possession,' she whispered, her huge

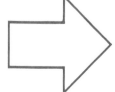

NO COST! NO OBLIGATION TO BUY! NO PURCHASE NECESSARY!

PLAY "LUCKY 7"
AND GET AS MANY AS SIX FREE GIFTS . . .

HOW TO PLAY:

1. With a coin, carefully scratch off the silver box at the right. This makes you eligible to receive one or more free books, and possibly other gifts, depending on what is revealed beneath the scratch-off area.

2. You'll receive brand-new Harlequin Presents® novels. When you return this card, we'll send you the books and gifts you qualify for *absolutely free!*

3. If we don't hear from you, every month we'll send you 8 additional novels to read and enjoy. You can return them and owe nothing but if you decide to keep them, you'll pay only $2.24* per book, a savings of 26¢ each off the cover price! There is *no* extra charge for postage and handling. There are no hidden extras.

4. When you join the Harlequin Reader Service®, you'll get our monthly newsletter, as well as additional free gifts from time to time just for being a member.

5. You must be completely satisfied. You may cancel at any time simply by sending us a note or a shipping statement marked "cancel" or returning any unopened shipment to us at our cost.

You'll love your elegant 20k gold electroplated chain! The necklace is finely crafted with 160 double-soldered links and is electroplate finished in genuine 20k gold. And it's yours free as added thanks for giving our Reader Service a try!

eyes on his angry face. 'I've never been anybody's possession. You frighten me! Please let me go!'

For a second he watched her with narrowed eyes that blazed into hers and then he let her go, straightening her clothes and watching her with all-knowing eyes before his hand came out to open the door.

He said nothing at all and she fled, racing up the path to the lodge, the second time that she had run from him here, her shaken mind reminded her. The flat was not yet sold, she would withdraw it from the agent. She just could not face Ben Shapiro again, she was helpless in his arms and now he knew it perfectly well.

CHAPTER SIX

TARA went to work the next day, her mind miserably admitting defeat. Her office looked the same, but she no longer felt the enthusiasm she had always felt for this job, this firm. She had been happy here, she mused, completely happy until Ben had started to force his way into her private life. She wished with all her heart that she could go back to those carefree days of work and travel. She never would now. She would always want more of Ben and never have it.

She looked up guiltily as Martin came into her office, expecting to see scorn, or at the very best blind rage. He was smiling ruefully and he made no attempt to come close.

'I'm sorry, Tara,' he said quietly. 'I behaved very badly last night. I did tell you that the green-eyed monster takes no fact into consideration. Shapiro has a good deal more sense than I have. He just let me drive off and it was the best thing. I came in this morning to resign but he explained. It was good of him after all I said.'

'He—he explained?' Tara got out in a strangled voice. What had he explained? That she was obsessed with him and that it was no good anyone else trying? She could just hear him arrogantly saying that!

'Yes. He told me about your mother and the operation, how it might—might leave her worse if things go wrong. I can see now why you became

98

hysterical and why he was holding you. God! I'm a real fool.'

Aren't we all? thought Tara bitterly. Ben could talk his way out of an avalanche!

'Anyway,' said Martin cheerfully, 'he pointed out that it would be a good idea to ease off the pressure on you at the moment. Funny, I hadn't realised that I was putting any pressure on you at all. Maybe I have, and in that case, I'm sorry. You know I only want what's best for you.'

Tara was stunned. Martin putting pressure on her! Ben Shapiro pressurised her to the point of exhaustion. As to Martin, it sounded too good to be true. She had not forgotten how she had instinctively felt aggression when he kissed her deeply. Her treacherous heart reminded her that she had felt no such thing when Ben kissed her, however angrily. Even last night when she had told him that she was afraid, it had been only partly true, her fear had been that she would not be able to resist him if he should become gentle in any way at all.

'I could do with a bit of help from you,' Martin was saying. 'Shapiro said you were the expert on presenting things in the best light for the firm. I have to work out some meetings on the Brazilian project. He thought you might give me a hand.'

Did he, now? After telling her that Martin would be waiting to murder her, he was quite prepared to throw her to the wolves if the firm was at stake. Still, it was her job, after all; she supposed she should be flattered that both men bowed to her judgement, although Martin had never asked her opinion before.

She galvanised herself into action, thrusting Ben's sinister cunning to the back of her mind, and soon she and Martin had their heads together discussing work, mapping out meetings, presentations and all the projects that would keep the name of IST to the front in Brazil. With no warning, Martin was different, quiet and gentle. It left her feeling extremely suspicious, as if the walls were closing in on her.

It was only after he had gone, a swift and brotherly kiss on the cheek his goodbye, that she had time to sit back and ask herself what kind of a situation Ben had worked her into. Last night she had been dismayed to find Mirry still up, Nurse Lewis wrapping up her inevitable knitting as she saw Tara come in.

'You're back early, dear!' Mirry had said with a close look at Tara's pale face. 'I suppose Ben has been having a little chat with you,' she said after Nurse Lewis had left.

Yes, you could say that, thought Tara miserably. Actually, he had been tying her into knots and she felt at that moment that it might take the rest of her life to unravel them.

'Yes,' she said aloud. 'I—I was a bit scared about the operation.'

'Don't be, darling,' her mother begged. 'I want to go ahead with it. I'm not the sort of person who can contemplate a life like this for ever, and I miss being able to move about. Sometimes I could scream.' She gave Tara a hug as she knelt down and put her arms around her. 'Mind you,' she added with a laugh that was just a little uneasy, 'if I had to wait a long time, I'm not sure I would have the courage to go ahead. I know the risks, but if I don't go ahead then I know too that I'm going to be regretting it for the rest of my life. Just so long as we can get it over with quickly.'

'Did Ben say anything about any waiting?' asked Tara in a calm, matter-of-fact voice.

'No. It's somebody he knows and apparently he'll do it at once if he thinks I can take it, and if he thinks it will be fairly safe. Ben's a miracle to me!' And a nightmare to me, thought Tara, but she knew what she had to do.

After Martin had gone, she walked like a sleepwalker to Ben's office and his eyes narrowed as he saw her come into the outer office as he was talking to Joan.

'Can I speak to you?' she asked quietly, her eyes looking through him, no expression in them at all.

'Come through into my office,' he said abruptly, taking her arm as if he felt that she would fall down. She was not too far off that, she conceded, and she sank thankfully into the chair he pulled out. It was the first time in her life that she had admitted defeat.

'I talked to Mirry,' she said in a calm voice, 'and she wants the operation, or at least, the chance of it. She's too scared to wait, though, for any list and spare bed. I'll do whatever you say.'

He was so still that she thought he had changed his mind, and she looked up at him anxiously.

'Tara,' he ground out, softly savage, 'I'm only wanting to help her! I knew how you'd take the offer, so I decided to offer you a job, an extra job. It's genuine enough. You were there last night. You're Public Relations. You know I need a hostess.'

'I still can't understand why Wanda . . .' she began quietly, but he cut across her remarks impatiently.

'Let her drop!' he said angrily. 'She can barely look after herself. As a hostess, she'd be the biggest liability I've got.'

'All right,' murmured Tara. 'It really doesn't matter at all.'

'What about Lambourne? Have you seen him?' asked Ben. 'I had a word with him this morning. I didn't know if he would come to see you.'

'Yes, I've seen him.'

Tara decided to let the whole matter drop. After all, she was now in a position where she could do nothing without Ben's approval and where he could say to her just about anything he liked.

He looked at her in exasperation.

'Well? What happened?' She didn't answer, and he added a little more quietly, 'Does he really matter to you, Tara?'

'I just feel that I've treated him badly, that any trouble he's in is all my fault and . . .'

'He's in no trouble at all,' Ben rasped. 'I can recognise jealousy when I see it. If he's going crazy for you, he has my sympathy. Oh, God, I didn't mean that!' He looked at his watch, flicking his sleeve back with an impatient gesture. 'It's lunch time. Come on!'

She didn't ask where and why, and this unusual submissiveness seemed merely to irritate him. It was only as he marched her to his car, Joan left with a list of orders, that Tara realised he had asked her out to lunch.

When they were settled in a quiet and rather dark restaurant, he brought up the subject of the operation.

'I've already made an appointment with Burgess. I know him personally and it seemed a good idea to get things moving.'

He stopped, looking as if he expected an outburst, and normally he would have got one at once. He had not consulted her about this and as far as she knew he had not consulted Mirry. No wonder he looked a trifle uneasy, Tara thought, but she was not in any frame of mind to battle. Maybe later she would get her sparkle back and put him in his place. Right now, she had no idea what his place was. They needed him, though, of that she was sure.

'Thank you,' she said quietly, looking intently at her hands folded in front of her on the table. 'She's a little scared, you know. I think that the sooner it's over and done with, the better.'

'How do you feel about it?' he asked cautiously.

'Scared. I couldn't face it if it made her worse, or if something—happened. She told me that she felt like screaming sometimes, did you know that? I had no idea. She keeps so cheerful and it's all a front. I should have known that. I should have seen.'

Her voice was rising, she knew, but at the moment she was at the end of her tether.

'Tara.' His hand closed over her tightly folded hands and she took a deep breath.

'I'm all right. Really I am. It's just that lately . . .'

'Have I done this to you?' he asked tightly. 'I had no intention of getting you into this state. What do I have to do to give back your spark?'

She looked up at him wonderingly and then slowly withdrew her hands.

'Nothing. You're just the same, after all. I'm the one who's different. I fully expect to recover. Let's talk about Mirry,' she said briskly, dismissing this soft way of speaking. It just didn't suit Ben and it didn't ring true either.

'I'd like to drive you both down to the hospital,' he

said, watching her face closely. 'I arranged for you to see Burgess there. His private rooms are a little awkward to approach. It would be better for Miriam to go to the hospital where things are all on one level.'

'If you think so,' Tara said evenly. 'It would be good for her morale to be able to go in style, but I doubt if the Ferrari . . .'

'I'll take her in style,' said Ben with a smile that threatened to get under her guard. 'I've got more than one car. Leave it to me.'

Tara nodded and then looked at him seriously.

'About paying.'

'Leave it, Tara!' Instantly he was annoyed, but she had no intention of leaving it.

'No, I can't leave it. Mirry and I had quite a talk last night. We have some money. I've been saving in case she needed anything, and this seems to be that occasion. It may not be enough but at least it will be a start. It all depends on what the final costs are.'

'Tara! There is no need to . . .' he began, but she had to get this all out right now and she interrupted firmly.

'This is what we've decided,' she said coolly. 'When we get the final costs, then we'll see. Anything extra and we will have to take up your offer. I'm quite prepared to—to act as your hostess then until the amount is paid off.'

'Do you have any idea how this is making me feel?' he demanded angrily, his amber eyes narrowed and piercing.

'I know how it's making me feel,' said Tara coldly. 'Mirry doesn't know anything about our—arrangement, and I'd be grateful if you wouldn't mention it.'

'In case she thinks that you're living with me to pay off the bill?' he bit out violently.

'She knows me better than that,' said Tara quietly, meeting his angry gaze. 'I'd better tell you the lot, while we're alone. If the operation is successful, then Mirry will probably want to move back to the city. I telephoned the agents this morning and withdrew the flat from their list.'

'How did you persuade Miriam into all this?' he asked impatiently. 'She never stops telling me how she loves the place.'

'I didn't persuade her,' Tara replied quietly. 'I pointed out that she would no longer be an invalid if it worked out. Perhaps someone who needs the lodge more would be able to have it then.'

'Didn't she point out to you that you're an ungrateful . . .' he began heatedly, but once again she interrupted, keeping her face cool by sheer willpower.

'You backed me into a corner,' she said softly, her dark tilted eyes on his angry face. 'You imagined a scenario and forced me into it. I don't dance to anyone else's tune, and as you pointed out a good while ago, I'm normally straightforward. When this is all over, for better or for worse, I shall leave IST. I won't be manoeuvred, I won't be harassed, sexually or otherwise, and in any case,' she added, looking away from his astonished eyes at last, 'I'm no longer happy there.'

There was a long pause and then he said shortly, 'Why?'

'You tell me,' she said softly, mocking his sardonic words to her. It robbed him of any last lingering

warmth, and the discussion carried on about the
hospital visit as if two strangers had met and been
forced into making mutually acceptable
arrangements.

He arrived in a long white Mercedes and came up to
fetch Miriam himself, placing her in the front of the
car and adjusting the seat for her comfort. It gave
Tara a small flip of tenderness towards him. She had
spent a good long time getting Mirry ready, helping
with her make-up, dressing her hair. It all helped the
morale, and Ben was treating her like a VIP. A small
smile softened Tara's face, but she quickly squashed it
as she looked up to see his eyes on her through the
rear-view mirror. He would find no chink in her
armour!

It was not difficult to be tight and silent as they
waited for her mother to return from the examination.
Tara paced restlessly about, not speaking, and Ben
seemed to be ignoring her too, reading a newspaper
with total concentration, as if this was a treat that he
rarely allowed himself.

Both their eyes were on Miriam, though, as a nurse
wheeled her back to the waiting-room, and she
couldn't wait to tell them.

'Mr Burgess thinks it will work!' her mother said
excitedly. 'There's a slight risk, but then we knew
that, and I've decided to go ahead.'

'When?' Tara knew she was almost whispering, but
the word 'risk' seemed to her to be mentioned a great
deal.

'In two weeks' time,' said Miriam. 'There's plenty
of time to prepare, and I want to get it over with

before I lose my nerve.'

She was treating it lightly, but Tara knew that she was scared. Whatever had to be done would be done. She could not ask what this would cost, all that had to be left to Ben. Tara suddenly realised that he was not there, he had gone in to see Mr Burgess. Maybe she was about to find out the cost, after all. In the event, he said nothing to either of them when he came out. His only thought seemed to be to cheer her mother along and get them safely back to the lodge.

There was a certain air of unreality about returning. Tara had the distinct feeling that they all felt it, although nobody said a word about the future. Ben kept up an entertaining flow of conversation with Miriam for the first few miles, but it was clear that Mirry was both excited and uneasy, and after a while they all fell silent.

Tara sat in a sort of nightmare. She was more anxious about her mother than she had admitted to herself, and with the certainty of the operation, the possibility of its success, time was running out for her. Soon, she would never see the lodge, the beautiful parkland and Ellerdale Manor again. She would never see Ben Shapiro again. From being a driving, ambitious person, she was now bewildered, admitting exactly how she felt about him. It had happened so fast that her mind would not properly accept it even now.

Things had been taken out of her hands again, even though she had been alerted to that possibility months ago. Now, with the prospect of her mother's complete recovery and with the thought of Ben constantly in her mind, she was like a ship with no helm, drifting helplessly, each day a day of waiting, her normal drive and energy drained away by emotion.

Her emotions were dangerously fragile now almost all the time, and there was more waiting yet, more endless worrying about the future. It would be wonderful to have her mother back on her feet, her old self again. What would Mirry want to do then, stay at Ellerdale Lodge? She would have to leave IST and escape from Ben. It was inevitable, because things would never be the same.

Everything looked clean, beautiful, as they drew up at the lodge, the world washed and bright after a shower of rain, and Tara saw her mother's eyes quickly scan the garden, the cottage and the tall trees of the woods. It almost made her heart stop beating. Mirry did not want to leave this beautiful place!

The journey had tired her, though, that and the tension, and Tara hurried her to her room, tucking her up in bed, knowing that Ben had not gone after he had seen Miriam to her door. It made her nervous, but she went out into the sitting-room and faced him squarely.

'Would you like a cup of tea?' she asked quietly, knowing that he would not. It was early afternoon and he would still have work to do at the office. She had taken the day off at his insistence.

He confounded her as usual.

'Thank you, I would. It's been a bit worrying. Still, we know the outcome now and can plan accordingly.'

Tara darted off to make the tea. She didn't quite feel up to facing Ben and his plans, he had too many of them.

She brought up the subject of risk when Miriam

was safely asleep and they were drinking their tea like a polite couple who had just met for the first time.

'How much risk is there?' she asked quietly. 'You went in to see Mr Burgess. No evasion, please.'

'No evasion,' he agreed, looking at her steadily. 'I'll tell you what he told me, as I explained to him that I was acting for you. This is an operation on the spine. Any operation there is risky. There is compression of the lower spine, to put it in layman's terms that you and I can understand, and it's going to be a delicate and skilful operation. The risk is that if it goes wrong, worse paralysis can occur, permanent paralysis. Miriam knows the risk, it was all explained to her, that's why she is so exhausted, I think—tension. But she wants to take the chance. Nobody has the right to try to dissuade her.'

'I wasn't going to,' Tara assured him, looking at her trembling hands. 'What do you think?' She looked up at him, her hands clenched in her lap.

'We have one life. We should live it as best we can, but we should live it to the full if possible, with the best quality of life we can attain. That's what I think. Miriam can attain better than she has now. She should go for it with all her heart.'

'Or die in the attempt!' said Tara in a dull voice.

'You wish that I'd never asked Burgess to see her?' Ben asked tightly, his face a little grim.

'No. I wouldn't blame you whatever happened,' Tara said quickly, her head shooting up. 'I know now how she feels about her disability. I thought she was reasonably happy, but she's not that at all. Whatever happens I'll always be grateful for the things you've done for her.'

'Helping Miriam is a privilege,' he said in a taut voice. 'You know how I feel about that.'

Yes, and about many other things, Tara thought, but aloud she said, 'Did you ask Mr Burgess about the cost of the operation?'

It removed his sombre mood like magic.

'I did not. I'm not accustomed to asking how much things cost. I wait for the bill.'

'The bill will be mine,' she said quietly and firmly, 'and unfortunately Mirry and I do have to ask the price of things!'

'Not this particular thing,' he rapped out in a low and vicious voice, anxious not to wake Miriam and have her know how mercenary her daughter was. 'You've already laid down the ground rules. I'll play by them.'

'Provided that we understand each other,' said Tara, not at all shaken by his anger. She was getting used to it, and her own anger was constantly simmering.

'Oh, I understand you all right,' Ben grated, getting to his feet and moving to the door. 'You, though, don't seem to understand me. My particular ship does not sink. Ponder on that.'

He walked off and she saw the Mercedes sweep out of the drive. He was going back to work. Let him! She would ponder on nothing at all. One step at a time, and the first step was to see that Mirry had her chance.

She took a week off work when the day came for Miriam to go into hospital. For herself, she would rather have been working to keep her mind off things, but she might be needed and she would stay close to her mother until this was all over.

'Will you stay in town or drive back to the lodge every day?' asked Ben when they were set to go.

He had insisted upon driving them down again, and his physical presence seemed to give her mother courage.

'I'll stay in town, of course,' said Tara. 'I could stay at the flat, but the furniture is almost all here at the lodge, so I've booked into a hotel close to the hospital.'

He nodded, and Tara had the annoying feeling that she had reported in to him and been given clearance to go ahead. She tightened her lips and kept silent, thinking unfairly that she would rather have paid for an ambulance to take them all the way.

He insisted upon going in with her later to sit with Miriam. The operation was the next afternoon, and he pointed out stiffly that Miriam wanted no grim faces around her, and she would have liked to point out to him that before he blew into her life she had never had a grim face at all.

For Miriam's sake though, Tara brightened up, but her face again fell when after a rather silent dinner at a very splendid restaurant, Ben dropped her off at her hotel and drove away without a backward glance.

The next day was a nightmare. She had been asked not to visit at all and the time stretched ahead like an unending road. She simply sat in her hotel room and watched the clock, unable either to read or do anything else. She dared not go out even for a minute in case something went wrong and they called for her.

When the telephone rang, she nearly cried out

aloud. It was Ben.

'Have you heard anything?' She knew that she was almost shouting, but there seemed to be nothing that she could do about it.

'Of course not,' he said quietly. 'It's far too early. You're to ring at six, you know that. I just wondered how things are with you there.'

'I—I'm all right,' she managed, although she was almost in tears. The constant waiting was wearing her down, and she had no one but herself to blame. She knew that if she had asked him he would have stayed here and waited with her. 'Have—have you been busy today?' she said, anxious to keep him talking, even comforted by the sound of his voice over the phone.

'I've got a few things done. Everyone knows, they're anxious for you. All being well, you should be able to visit tomorrow, see her for yourself.'

'All being well,' Tara repeated unhappily.

'Is it getting you down there, Tara?' he asked astutely, hearing the misery in her voice. 'Shall I collect you?'

She automatically said no, self-preservation being a strong feeling at all times.

'I can't leave the telephone,' she said more sharply than she intended, and to her dismay he simply cut her off. She found herself looking at a dead phone and wishing that things were different. She needed him. She admitted that openly.

She went back to watching the clock, more miserably now than before, and her heart leapt right up in her throat when there was a sharp tap on her door. She almost tore the door open, stunned to see Ben there, his face grim as he looked down at her.

'Get your things,' he said firmly. 'You're going out for a while.'

'I can't leave the . . .'

'Telephone messages can quite easily be re-routed,' he said ironically. 'I have already given my car phone number at the desk and impressed upon them that this is an emergency. We'll get the call, if one comes!'

Tara didn't doubt that, and she was so filled with relief to see him that she simply picked up her bag and coat and followed him.

'Where are we going?' she asked in a small voice as he grimly drove in and out among the traffic.

'I have a flat in town. I'm staying there tonight and every night until Miriam is out of all danger. We're going there.'

'I—I can't! I don't want . . .'

'You don't want to be seduced? I can understand that,' he said scathingly. 'Wait until you're asked, Miss Frost.'

She fell into gloomy silence, feeling gauche and ridiculous, and he glanced at her after a while, his face quite still and serious.

'You, my dear young lady, are going to sleep,' he said firmly, no give at all in his voice. 'Miriam does not need a gibbering wreck to look at when she comes round. You are going to pull yourself together and I am going to make quite sure that you do.'

She looked up in whirl of anxiety, but he ignored her and drove on. Apparently she had no alternative.

His flat was in a beautiful curving Georgian crescent, the sort of place that showed how very beautiful the city could be. Their own flat had been large and expensive, and this gave Tara some vague

idea of the cost of a place like this. The interior was no
disappointment, either. Ben was a very wealthy man
and lived like one. She felt in an even greater state of
nerves.

He walked across the deeply carpeted hall, clearly
expecting her to follow, but Tara was too engrossed
by the pictures in gilt frames, the beautiful lacquered
Chinese cabinet, the long white settee that she could
see through the door of the sitting-room. As a flat, this
was a palace. It was more than ever unbelievable that
he should have taken an interest in their lives.

'This way,' he was saying quietly, his eyes keenly
on her as she stood feeling stranded and alone. 'This is
the room you can use. Put your coat and things in
here and I'll make us some coffee, then we'll think
about eating, unless you've already had lunch.'

All she could do was shake her head foolishly. It
now seemed like madness to have actually left her
hotel with him. She knew what he could do to her
with just a glance. It was luxurious and quiet. The
city might have been miles away. It was an oasis of
richly gilded peace, packed with danger. She knew
that her steps were dragging, her feet reluctant to take
her towards him, and not for the life of her could she
meet his eyes.

'I'll leave you to it,' he said tightly, not that his
anger surprised her, for she was behaving like a fool.
'Come into the sitting-room when you're ready. The
coffee will be there by then.' He walked off, making it
possible for her to enter the room without the
necessity of passing close to him, and she closed the
door behind her, her heart beating madly.

This was ridiculous! In her need for him she had

imagined that he would simply take her out to lunch, sit down and talk about Mirry. That now seemed to be a foolish idea. He never did anything normal!

She stood and looked at herself in the long, elegant mirror. Her face was pale, strained with worry about her mother, her eyes dark-shadowed with lack of sleep. She no longer looked like the healthy, vigorous person who had started work at IST so long ago. No wonder he had asked her how could he give back her spark!

There was nothing she could do about it. At least she was wearing a nice dress, a very demure little thing in peach, but it clung in all the right places, hugging her waist and flaring out into a full skirt, the bodice buttoned and pretty, emphasising her round breasts. She took off her pale, lightweight coat, brushed her hair and walked in to face Ben, hoping that he realised just how very demure she was, her heart thumping away like a jungle drum.

CHAPTER SEVEN

'JUST in time!' He was walking into the drawing-room with a laden tray, and he set it down on the coffee-table, seemingly as intent on avoiding her gaze as she had been to avoid his. 'Sit down, Tara. I hope you're not going to stand on ceremony here. Treat the place as your own and try to relax a little.'

'Thank you.' She sat on the settee, forcing herself to sit back and not perch on the edge as if prepared for flight. He was right about one thing, she was tightened up inside to an extent that she had not realised.

She seemed unable to take her eyes off him. He had taken off his jacket and loosened his tie, his powerf l shoulders tightening the shirt as he leaned forward to pour the coffee. He probably thought that she would have dropped everything, and he was probably right.

'Here we are,' he said quietly, handing her a cup, speaking as if she were about six years old, or dangerously mad. His voice was deliberately soothing, and she knew that he was trying to be kind, that he knew how frightened she was for Mirry. Once again he had come to the rescue.

'I suppose you're wondering if I can get any message here,' he asked, looking at her over the rim of his cup. 'I can, I've now transferred all hospital calls to here. Any other worries?' he asked, his eyes now on her downcast face.

'No, except the usual one. How is she, will she be all right?'

'That we'll know when they tell us,' he said steadily. 'Assuming that she will be, I really would like to see you in better shape to face the visiting tomorrow.'

He was silent for a moment when she simply nodded and then he added quietly, 'You can stay here instead of the hotel if you want to, Tara. You're very much alone there.'

'Oh, no! I'm fine there. I—I like being alone.'

There was a great deal of anxiety on her face and he grimaced in sudden exasperation, putting his cup down and standing abruptly.

'You're perfectly all right here, just as long as we can dodge around each other and think only of Miriam. The fact that you're behaving as if you're about to be savaged is, I hope, merely a temporary attack of nerves.' He glared down at her and then walked to the door. 'I'll make you something to eat.' There was an abrasive quality in his voice that showed how irritated he was under this soothing exterior.

'No, thank you,' she said urgently. 'I couldn't eat a thing. I—I'm too—too . . .'

'Uptight is the word you're looking for,' he said, coming back and reaching for her hand. 'Come along, then. I brought you here to see that you get some sleep. That's exactly what you're going to do.'

'I want to wait for the hospital to phone.' She sat perfectly still, with no intention of moving, a squeal of alarm leaving her startled lips when he bent and scooped her up into his arms.

'Don't make the mistake of fighting me,' he said in

a mocking voice. 'You just don't have the height.
Sleep, I said, and sleep it's going to be. I shall stay
here and wait for any calls. The decisions have been
made. All you have to do is try to obey for once.'

'Then you can put me down, thank you,' Tara
managed tightly. 'I'm quite capable of walking to the
bedroom, and I won't be making a run for the street.'

'What an undignified thought,' he mocked,
ignoring her request, walking through into the
bedroom where she had left her coat, and dumping
her unceremoniously on the bed. 'There we are! Off
with the dress and shoes, into bed like a good girl and
you'll be back to normal in no time.'

He walked out, closing the door and leaving her
glaring angrily after him. The anger didn't last long,
however. The tiredness she had been holding off
seemed to grow as the soft bed beckoned, and she did
exactly as she had been told, slipping off her dress and
shoes and sliding under the covers. She felt as if a
weight had been lifted from her mind and her lips
curved in an unwilling smile as she closed her eyes. In
spite of everything, he was very good to her. She
wanted to cling to him and never let go.

It was dark when she woke up, and it was not just
because the curtains were closed. Oddly enough she
knew exactly where she was and the first thought that
came into her head was about her mother. Ben had
left the flat! He had not called the hospital! She kicked
back the covers, ready to race out into the other room.

'Hold everything!' He was just walking in, a cup of
tea in his hand, his finger flicking a switch that
brought the lamps on around the room, and she

hastily slid back under the covers.

'Ben!' she said accusingly. 'I've slept through it all, it's the middle of the night!'

'Wrong twice,' he corrected, placing the tea on the bedside-table and sitting beside her, his brilliant eyes on her face.

'It's only eight thirty, you've slept through nothing and I've just phoned the hospital.' He smiled into her anxious eyes and did not keep her waiting. 'She's out of the theatre, resting quietly, and the operation seems to have been a success.'

'Seems?' Tara tightened her hands on the sheets and looked at him with a desperate intensity.

'I spoke to Burgess himself,' he told her softly. 'Before the operation she was given a few orders that she would remember in spite of being still a bit far gone when she came round. The orders were "move your toes" and then "move your feet". She did both! So far, Burgess is delighted. He thinks that she'll be able to walk!'

'Walk!' Tara stared at him, her eyes filled with happy tears, and then she threw her arms around his neck and buried her face against him. 'Oh, Ben!' She burst into healing tears and his arms locked around her, holding her as she wept the tension and anxiety away.

For a while she forgot where she was, forgot exactly who was holding her so tightly. When she did remember, she drew away, flushing with embarrassment.

'I'm sorry,' she sniffed, looking anywhere but at him. 'I don't normally go to pieces.'

'I know,' he said emphatically, laughter in his voice.

'Let's call it an unexpected treat.' His golden eyes
flared over her as she looked at him in a startled
manner, not knowing exactly what he meant. 'Tea,
madam,' he said softly, handing her her cup. 'Drink
this, get dressed and we'll go out and celebrate.'

He stood and walked to the door and stopped only
when she said quietly, 'Ben. Thank you!'

'Any time,' he assured her in a curiously intense
voice. 'Hurry up and we'll paint the town.'

He walked out and she found herself staring at the
door, at the place where he had been a few seconds
ago. Her eyes opened wide, as if seeing things clearly
for the first time ever. She really loved that irritating,
domineering man! The thought brought with it the
picture of Wanda and phantoms of unseen, unknown
other women—of his wife who still probably held his
heart; but it did nothing to sadden her. For the
moment she was simply hugging her new-found
knowledge to herself. It was like a light that had
suddenly come on in a dark room.

She kept her thoughts strictly to herself and
behaved as normally as possible, but it could not help
but colour her behaviour, and several times she found
Ben's eyes intently on her as the evening progressed.
She had been adamant that she did not wish to go
anywhere splendid, and he had found a small
restaurant tucked away behind the main streets.

It was dimly lit and cosy and the food was superb.
Tara found that she was starving and she ate her way
through everything put before her, talking animatedly
about Miriam and the future as Ben watched and
made suitable comments, his eyes on her unusual,
expressive face.

It was only as she sat back and had yet another glass of wine that she realised just how much she had talked and just how much she had eaten. It brought a blush to her already flushed cheeks.

'I've been eating and talking for ages,' she said in a quiet, horrified voice.

'It's been a pleasure to watch,' he assured her, laughing openly at her embarrassment. 'Just so long as it doesn't fuel your temper!'

'Oh, I couldn't be bad-tempered tonight,' Tara sang out gaily. 'I'm deliriously happy! I could go on all night!'

'It's two minutes past midnight,' said Ben softly, 'and you may not have noticed in this happy state, but they've closed the restaurant around us.'

'Oh, how awful!' Tara giggled, her hand coming to her mouth as she realised something else. She had drunk her way through a great deal of wine, and Ben had sat there and let her.

'I think you'd better take me to my hotel,' she said with exaggerated dignity, making an effort to stand, and he was instantly on his feet, his hand under her arm, his grin only just hidden.

When the outside air hit her she was more dizzy than ever, the tendency to giggle very pronounced, but Ben coaxed her to his car, fastened her securely in, and she closed her eyes with a feeling of great gratitude. She hadn't a worry in the world.

The sound of the car door slamming and the cool air on her face roused her, and it dawned on her immediately that they were not at her hotel. It was too quiet for that.

'Where is this?' she asked with an attempt at an

aloof question that didn't quite come off.

'My flat,' said Ben evenly, his voice very matter-of-fact as he helped her out of the car and up the steps. That seemed to make everything all right.

'Jolly good,' she said merrily, missing the step and giggling as he swung her up into his arms.

He didn't bother with the light in the hall, but simply made straight for the room she had used before. It was then that a faint anxiety hit her.

'Ben,' she said anxiously as he switched on the lamps and carried her towards the bed, 'you won't . . . ?'

'Not without due warning, kitten,' he said soothingly. 'I'm never sneaky.'

She began to laugh softly and couldn't stop.

'I bet you are!' she burbled, and then passed out completely.

Sunlight was streaming into the room when she awoke and she looked round the room, her puzzled gaze falling on her dress, her shoes and her slip. She didn't need to look to know that she was in her panties and bra, and she also knew that she had not undressed herself. She was sitting with the sheets to her chin, her knees drawn up and a very worried expression on her face as Ben walked in.

'Why, you're awake!' he said in surprise. 'I expected to have to shake you. I just phoned the hospital and Miriam is in good shape. She had a comfortable night and we can see her this evening, but not before. She has to see Burgess and whole battery of other people and get some rest today. I sent her a message from you.'

Bossy, bossy, bossy! Tara thought darkly, but aloud she said very quietly, 'Thank you.'

'Anything else?' he asked quietly, his eyes on her rather troubled face.

'I'm sorry about last night,' she said in a subdued voice. 'I expect I made an utter idiot of myself.'

'You were quite delightful,' he assured her softly, coming slowly forward. 'How's the head this morning?'

'I feel fine!' she said, and oddly enough she did.

He tutted and looked at her accusingly. 'Hard-drinking female? I would never have guessed it.'

'I've never done that before,' Tara protested quickly. 'I can't think what came over me.'

'I suppose it was my fault,' he confessed with no sign of remorse. 'I wanted you to relax. You entered into the spirit of things wholeheartedly, however. I must admit it took me by surprise. I expected a certain amount of opposition.'

'I—I passed out,' Tara mumbled, the sheets tightly around her chin. 'I'm sorry that you had to—had to . . .'

'Undress you? Get it out! It's nothing to worry about. I assure you that I treated you like an inanimate object, which you were, almost,' he added with a low laugh.

'You've been very good to me,' said Tara in an almost accusing voice, and his eyebrows shot up quizzically.

'Searching the far reaches of my mind, I can't remember when I wasn't good to you, or trying to be against fierce opposition,' he said mildly.

'I'm sorry,' she murmured, and his hand closed

around her chin, tilting her face up.

'Keep on fighting,' he advised quietly. 'I assure you it's the wisest thing. I'm no angel.'

'I'm beginning to think that you are,' she confessed guilelessly, and he stood abruptly, his face hardening suddenly, although he smiled at her.

'It's nice to be appreciated. Get dressed and come and eat. I'll take you back to your hotel then, because I have to get to work.'

It all dawned on her as he left. He still thought she was throwing herself at him and he still didn't like it at all. He had been merely kind. She was the one with the love hanging around her neck like a millstone.

She washed and dressed quickly, her mind made up, and she walked into the kitchen with the old determined look on her face.

'If you'll drop me off at the hotel, I'll get a quick shower and change and then I'm coming to work,' she said firmly. 'I can't see Mirry until tonight. She's out of danger. I may as well work.'

'There's no need,' he began, his eyes narrowing at the changed expression on her face, but she cut in decidedly.

'I want to. I can't hang around with time on my hands! I've got plenty to do at work and it will all pile up while I'm off. I'll probably need some time off when Mirry gets home, and I'd like to keep up to date.'

'Very well,' he said quietly, pushing her breakfast across to her. 'Career woman first to last. I'll wait for you and drive you in.'

That seemed to be the end of any conversation, and she couldn't tell at all what it was that had taken the smile from his eyes, but she imagined it was her softened attitude in the bedroom. After all, she mused, if he could undress her and put her to bed and have no lingering thoughts about it, then he clearly wasn't interested. Her face flooded with colour at this erotic thought, and she hoped he hadn't noticed her change of expression. He was eating sombrely and he had noticed nothing.

Everyone wanted to know how her mother was. Tara was very popular and everyone in the city office had been shocked at the accident that had killed her father and left her mother paralysed. Now they seemed to be willing her on, and Tara's spirits rose at all this kindness.

Martin was out of the office this morning, seeing his contacts in the city, and she was a little relieved at that. His outburst at Ben's house had quite frightened her, and since then he had been a little odd, startling her by watching her when she wasn't looking, his face changing rapidly as she caught his eye. What had begun as a pleasant friendship and developed into a quiet relationship with no passion on her part had got out of hand. She would be glad when he was back in Brazil and had time to forget about her.

At lunch time she was in the main body of the building chasing up some notes and her heart sank at the sight of Ben going out to lunch, Wanda Pettigrew firmly beside him, laughing up into his face. She was surprised how much it hurt. Before it had merely made her angry and then jealous, now it actually hurt like a pain inside. She missed lunch and worked on, drowning her sorrows in being busy, trying to push him out of her mind.

It was almost five when Martin came back and he caught sight of her as he passed her office.

'Tara!' He came straight in and hovered over her. 'I thought you were off until your mother was out of hospital.'

'No, I can't sit around. I decided to come in because I can't visit until tonight.'

She smiled up at him and he looked puzzled.

'When was the operation, then? I thought you were visiting last night. I rang your hotel about nine to see how things were and just got the message that you would be out until further notice.'

'Oh!' Tara smiled and shook her head, her next words completely thoughtless. 'I was at Ben's flat. I went there during the early afternoon.'

She knew just what she had said and how it looked as soon as the words were out of her mouth, but even so she was not prepared for his reaction.

'You little slut!' He grabbed her arms, yanking her to her feet, holding her in front of him. 'I knew it! As soon as I saw you with him at his house, I knew it! All this talk of helping your mother. You're one of his women, aren't you?'

Tara opened her mouth to protest at this manhandling, at his insulting remarks, but she had no time to speak, her temper lost in fright at the sight of his face. He seemed to have gone quite mad, and he began to shake her violently, his hands then tightening around her neck as he shook her more.

It was Bob Carter who dragged him away from her, the Personnel Officer's sheer bulk enough to throw Martin against the wall as Tara collapsed into her seat, her head in her hands. Everything was swimming. Her throat was burning where his fingers had been, and she had never felt so close to fainting in her life.

'Tara!' Ben was there when she opened her eyes. He was crouched down beside her chair, looking up into her face, his own face white with fury. 'It's all right, he stormed out of the building,' he said furiously as she looked anxiously around. 'Bob came for me. Can you stand?'

When she nodded, he put his arm around her and helped her to his office, and she was too shaken to feel any embarrassment as she noticed that half the people in the main office were staring at them with shocked expressions on their faces. Clearly they had heard the tirade that Martin had hurled at her.

Joan was on her feet as they came in, and Ben shook his head at her warningly. 'Hold any calls and get ready with the tea in about three minutes,' he said quietly. 'Just give her a little while to calm down.'

He let her sit for a minute in his office, leaning against the desk close to her, his eyes on her bent head.

'What happened?' he said quietly after a while. 'What made him blow his top like that? Bob Carter said he was like a lunatic.'

'He rang my hotel last night and I wasn't there. They told him that I would be out until further notice.

'That's the message I left for anyone who wasn't hospital,' Ben agreed. 'He went mad at that?' he asked in amazement.

'No. I—I wasn't thinking. I was so busy and—I told him I was at your flat.'

'I see!' Ben said slowly. '*Then* he went mad! How did he come to know the hotel you were staying at?' he asked tightly. 'Do you have to report your whereabouts to him all the time?'

She could hardly believe his harsh tones when she felt so sick with fright, and she looked up into his angry eyes, her temper flaring.

'No, I don't! I left it at the main switchboard in case anyone wanted me. But even if I did, it would be nothing to do with you! I'm sick and tired of people thinking they own me! I go out with Martin a few times and he imagines he has the right to demand explanations, to treat me like this! And you,' she added violently, 'you're worse! You don't even care, but you think you can say and do just whatever you like!'

Tara burst into tears, her hands around her aching neck, and he pulled her up into his arms, holding her tightly to him as she struggled.

'Don't fight, Tara, not this time,' he said quietly. 'I asked for that, and by God I surely got it. Don't cry, everything's going to be just fine!'

'Don't patronise me!' she sobbed. 'I'm not a child! I'm as clever as you any day!'

'You surely are,' he murmured softly, wiping her tears, and she glanced up to glare at him, not at all certain that this too was not patronising.

'Let's nip round to the pub and get you a brandy,' he suggested, straightening her up and reaching for his jacket. 'We'll skip the tea. It's time to shut up shop here, anyway.'

Joan had stayed but the rest of the staff seemed to have gone, and Tara collected her coat and bag, dazed and shocked still, feeling so unreal that she simply went with Ben and made no move to assert herself further.

'Now, you listen to me,' he said quietly when they were settled in a dark corner, the hubbub of noise giving them privacy. 'This is not the last of Lambourne as far as you're concerned. There's no way I'm letting you go back alone to that hotel when he's somewhere out there roaming around feeling badly done by.'

'He wouldn't . . .' Tara began anxiously, her eyes still wet with tears.

'He did!' Ben said determinedly, his strong hand covering hers. 'I'm taking you back there now and you're going to pack while I wait for you. Do you hear me, Tara?'

'Yes.' She nodded, and he sighed and leaned back. 'Well, that's a relief! I normally get a long speech when I offer ideas. Drink your brandy and we'll be on our way. There's Miriam to visit tonight, and you'll want to get into better shape before you see her. You can get ready at your hotel while I wait. We'll visit straight from there and then we'll have dinner. Don't ask me to let you out of my sight, because I have no intention of so doing.'

'Thank you,' said Tara quietly, and he suddenly laughed.

'Wonders,' he said, 'will never cease! A submissive Miss Frost! This must be a record!'

'I know when I'm licked,' she said dully, her head down, her eyes filling again with tears.

'That day will never come,' he said quietly, his hand reaching for her as he pulled her to her feet. 'This is merely a temporary setback. Tonight you'll be safe, tomorrow I'll get rid of Lambourne and the day after you'll be as irritating as ever.'

'I don't want you to fire him,' said Tara desperately, still feeling that this was in some way her fault.

'Please, Tara,' he said mockingly, 'let me run my own firm! You've ordered me out of your life, warned me off from interfering, accused me of being chauvinistic. Can I run my own firm, please?'

She found herself laughing, and his arm came round her to give her an unexpected hug.

'You'll never be licked,' he said softly. 'No wonder I refuse to fire you, you're unique!'

And one hundred per cent foolish, thought Tara sadly, struggling hard not to melt against him and spoil everything. He was just a man with well-developed protective instincts, a first class guardian angel. Anyone else who had the same sort of trouble that she had would find him right there, willing and ready to help. He was well worth loving, but she wished that she didn't love him quite so much.

He waited in the foyer of the hotel while she changed and packed, and the thought that he had probably paid her bill ran irritatingly through her head all the time. He hadn't. It gained him a pleasant smile which he seemed to find both puzzling and amusing, and that fact brought to Tara's mind the realisation that he had no idea just how domineering he was.

It was with a great deal of misgiving that Tara visited her mother. She was glad of Ben's presence, completely overlooking the fact that he had not for one minute considered the possibility of not accompanying her. He had arranged this, had taken charge, and as far as she could see he meant to play it through to the end.

Miriam was awake and utterly unmoving, her eyes turned to the window as they walked into the quiet room. For a moment, Tara's heart lurched with fear and Ben's hand came warningly to her shoulder, but Miriam turned her head on hearing them, and every bit of tension drained away as she smiled that same old smile across at her daughter.

'Would you believe it,' she said brightly, 'I can move my toes?' They both stood quite still, watching her, and she added ruefully, 'At the moment, I can't quite wiggle them, but I'm working on that!'

'Oh, Mirry!' Tara flew across to her, taking her hand and raising it to her face, kissing the pale fingers. 'You're so brave! I've been in a panic, and here you are, perfectly calm.'

'Well done, Miriam!' said Ben quietly and deeply, taking her other hand and looking down at her. 'I think we've all managed quite well, all things considered.'

'If it hadn't been for you two, I wouldn't have gone through with it. Do you realise that, Ben?' said Miriam quietly, looking up into his handsome face. 'Now I know that I'll be able to walk again. I owe such a lot to both of you for your encouragement and enthusiasm. Tara has always been like that, a tiny little dynamo, but I never thought that there would be someone else to help her in her attempts to boost my courage!'

It was terrible, the way Mirry bracketed them together! She was always doing it! How many times had she referred to them as 'you two'? It must be an embarrassment to Ben.

Tara stole a look at him, but he was smiling down at her mother as if it had all washed over him, and Tara felt a burst of contrary anger. Maybe he was so accustomed to interfering in the lives of other people that he was used to this. It wasn't fair to think that, but she thought it.

'We want to see you up and about, Miriam,' said Ben with one of his smiles that always charmed her mother. 'I've never seen you mobile. Tara must have got her drive and energy from somewhere, and I suspect that it was from you.'

'Let's hope that I don't disappoint you,' said Miriam with a laugh. 'It's going to be some time yet!'

Then I'll be leaving IST, thought Tara desperately. When her mother was better they would move away from Ellerdale. She could never again face seeing Ben without his love. She forced a smile to her lips as she found Ben's eyes intent on her. He missed nothing, and this was something he must never find out.

'When will you be out?' she asked brightly, her face colouring as Ben continued to stare at her with those brilliant eyes.

'According to this morning's consultation, not for some time, darling,' said Mirry regretfully. 'I've been immobile for a long time and the legs need a great deal of encouragement to walk again. They have all the facilities here and I shall stay. I don't want you staying at the lodge by yourself,' she added firmly.

'I'm keeping an eye on her,' said Ben with equal firmness, and Miriam looked up sharply, her dark eyes meeting his clear gaze.

'I rely on you a lot, don't I?' She watched him for a moment and he grinned down at her.

'The firm takes care of its own,' he assured her evenly. 'No need for worries. Anything else troubling you, Miriam?'

'Not that I can think of,' she laughed, looking greatly pleased. 'I leave her to you, then!'

'Thank you! I don't find her all that much of a burden,' he said softly. 'You'll probably discover that she's all in one piece when you get out.'

For a moment his eyes met Tara's. He had told her very strictly to wear a high scarf for this visit. The marks of Martin's fingers were now quite pronounced. If she wasn't all in one piece it would not be Ben's fault but her own inability to judge character. He was pointing that out to her very craftily. It made her temper flare.

'I have been known to take care of myself from time to time,' she said with as much sarcasm as she could, in view of her mother's presence.

'But why should you?' Ben asked quietly, his eyes back to irony. 'Two heads are better than one, they say, and we get on famously, don't we?'

'Beautifully,' said Tara with a brilliant smile that must have fooled Mirry because she sighed contentedly.

'Well, then,' she murmured comfortingly, 'that's nice!'

Ben's eyes moved to Tara's face, roaming over her rather fragile beauty, the way she had become lately, and she suddenly felt the need to avoid that probing gaze yet again. Unexpectedly, her eyes were warm with tears. Miriam accepted everything that Ben told

her, she always had done. There wasn't a woman alive
who could escape his magnetism, the spell of those
golden eyes. She felt brittle, ready to run away, far
and fast. Ready to quit for the first time in her life.

'Time to leave, I'm afraid.' A nurse came in,
smiling but firm, her eyes widening as she saw Ben,
and Tara bent to kiss her mother swiftly. If she stayed
near to Ben, continuing to work for him, living in the
lodge, it would always be like this, women falling all
over him, the new-found pain of it growing every day.

'I'll see you tomorrow, Mirry,' she promised
huskily, desperate now to be alone when she had
wanted company so badly before: Ben's company!
Now she couldn't get away fast enough.

'I have to book into a new hotel now,' she said flatly
and coldly as they reached the outside. 'You can leave
me here, I'll take a taxi.'

'No trouble, I'll drive you,' he said smoothly. 'Your
suitcase is already in the car, shame to bother with a
taxi when I'm here and quite willing to act the part.'

'Thank you,' said Tara stiffly. This was the last
time, the very last time that he would be allowed to
make a move in her life. She could not afford to be in
any way relaxed with him. One false move and he
would know that all he had suspected, all he had
accused her of was quite correct. If he pointed out just
once more that she wanted him, she would probably
scream that she did at the top of her voice.

CHAPTER EIGHT

TARA was so locked inside her own gloom that she failed to pay any attention to the drive. Ben would know an hotel, and this last once she would leave it to him. She would permit herself this final indulgence, pretend that she belonged to him, that he cared for her. This euphoric state was quickly dispelled, however, when he drew up outside his own flat and switched off the engine.

'Why are we here?' she asked sharply into the suddenly frightening silence.

'Your hotel,' he said determinedly, opening the door and coming round to take her arm in one of his steel-like grips. 'This is where you're staying, at least for now.'

'I am not!' Tara was hauled out, but she was by no means a willing captive. 'Wild horses wouldn't get me in there!'

'There being none present,' he murmured, 'I'll have to see what I can do. Before you begin to take up an even more aggressive stance, let me point out that I have every intention of getting a good night's sleep. I cannot do that with an easy mind knowing as I do that Lambourne is still roaming around muttering furiously to himself.'

'He has no idea where I am,' Tara snapped, attempting to free herself.

'I'm taking no chances on his finding out.'

'I will not be kept under your wing!' Tara told him, her voice rising, and he glared down at her, not at all amused.

'You'll be taken in under my arm if you stand here arguing much longer,' he grated, 'and the general populace can think what they damned well like!'

The proximity of the general populace became embarrassingly obvious as Tara saw three people gazing at them with interest from across the road. She knew that he meant it too. He just didn't care what people thought. Better to go in and argue there. She snatched her arm free and walked with a suffering dignity up the steps to his front door.

She had never intended to be back here, she thought wildly, as the front door closed behind them. There was an evening and a night before her. Escaping was necessary, even if he thought she was certifiable. She watched him walk determinedly to her room and put her suitcase inside. She would wait until they were having dinner and then she would bring the matter up again. She would tell him that she was embarrassed, worried about her reputation, about what Mirry would think if she found out. He would see her point of view.

He did not. Over the meal he listened carefully and then said that tomorrow would be a good day to think about it, for tonight he had no idea where Lambourne was and he had no intention of letting her out of his sight. Short of leaping up and running, without her suitcase, there was little that Tara could do, and she simply kept quiet, her apparent annoyance bringing a grim look to his face that she would rather not have seen there.

They got in rather late and Tara went straight to her room. His present mood did not invite bright chatter and she had never felt less like that in her life. She didn't feel like sleep, either. There were too many things in her head that were disturbing and miserable.

If he had only left her alone, allowed her to be just another employee, ignored her need for help, she would never have felt like this, never have known that she loved him. It had not been some great, heart-lifting, love-at-first-sight feeling, it had grown on her steadily, forced further forward by his kisses, even by his anger, reinforced by the care he showed when she needed it most.

She gave up any idea of sleep, getting out of bed and slipping into her dressing-gown, envying Ben his ability simply to close his door and fall asleep. Perhaps a hot drink would help. She went silently on bare feet to the kitchen and raided the fridge with no misgivings.

'It's you, pottering around! I thought we had a visitor.'

Ben's voice from the doorway had her jumping guiltily and she looked around to see him standing there, still dressed, his jacket and tie discarded, his shirt partly unbuttoned.

'I thought you were asleep. Sorry, I couldn't sleep, I thought perhaps a drink . . . You haven't got any Horlicks,' she said almost accusingly.

'I feel that might just be a point in my favour,' he said with a grin. 'I'll have a milky coffee, and don't point out that it will keep me awake! You have a definite "grandma" look about you!'

He stood exactly where he was until she had the

drinks made, and her hands trembled more by the minute. He said not a word. When she handed him his drink, though, and made to take hers to bed, he took her cup and said quietly, 'Let's take them into the sitting-room. You're quite respectable,' he added when she looked down at her bedtime attire in a fluster.

It was impossible to make any kind of conversation. She was so busy trying to avoid looking at him, to keep her newly discovered feelings well hidden, that even the slightest remark was fraught with danger. He didn't seem to mind, though. He sat in a chair, his head thrown back, his eyes half closed, and Tara curled up on the settee, sitting almost bolt upright, her feet drawn neatly beneath her, her hands tight on the hot cup.

She put it down at last and saw that he had done the same. Neither of them had said so much as a word and the atmosphere was singing with tension. At least it was to her, he was probably half asleep. She moved a little stealthily to get up and go and instantly his eyes opened, his intent amber gaze on her, freezing her to the spot.

'Such a neat little thing,' he murmured quietly. 'That settee quite swallows you up. How you managed to get yourself up there seems a miracle.'

'I—I'm not that small,' Tara said nervously. 'I can see that you're prone to exaggeration!'

He ignored that and just went on looking at her until she looked hastily away.

'Come and sit here,' he commanded softly, looking seriously across at her. It frightened her out of her wits. She jumped up and grabbed her cup, uncertain what to do, realising that she was about to flee and not liking the idea at all. She was almost twenty-five, for goodness' sake, not a fifteen-year-old schoolgirl, no matter what he thought.

'I'll take the cups and wash them out,' she said firmly, marching across to get his, her very expression saying that she would stand no nonsense. He sat back watching her, a faint smile on his lips, his eyes intently on her flushed and anxious face, and as she bent to get his cup his fingers locked around her wrist, his other hand deftly removing her cup from her suddenly nerveless grasp.

'You never obey orders,' he complained softly. 'I said, come here.'

With one quick movement he unbalanced her, laughing softly at her scared little sound as she felt herself falling. There wasn't far to fall and she knew he would catch her. That was what scared her most.

'All right,' he said cynically, 'let's get it over with.'

'Don't, Ben!'

'Be quiet!' he said urgently, pulling her across his knees, his arms tightly around her, his hand in her hair securing her head. 'We both know that you've been waiting for this, whatever your sharp little tongue says. It seems so long since last time.'

He kissed her impatiently, implacably, his mouth almost hostile, his arms too tight, and there was a fast burst of fear that made her resist, but he ignored that, utterly unbending and hard.

Even so, the magic hit her, the enchantment growing to stifle her fear, until her hands found his shoulders, a blaze of rapture flooding every part of her, melting her towards him, turning his angry kiss into something entirely different.

His mouth moved over hers with a drowsy hunger, slowly and druggingly, until she was soft and pliant in his arms, too filled with ecstasy to have any fear when he lifted her, moving across to the settee to come down beside her, cradling her against him.

She felt his hands firm and warm against her ankles, moving over her legs before coming back to gather her close, his lips still searching hers with that deep, exciting movement, an invitation to temptation.

Now, the hands that had gripped her so hard caressed her, moving over her until she was in a trance-like state, bewitched, slender and warm in his arms.

'Are you frightened, kitten?' he asked huskily when at last he looked down into her face.

'No,' she whispered, her face glowing, her head on the dark, velvet cushion that was a perfect setting for her fair, disordered hair.

'Then maybe we should stop while we're still in control of the situation,' he suggested softly, his eyes warming as she looked up at him ardently, her disappointment plain to see. 'Oh, Tara!' he murmured softly. 'You're so very hard to control and impossible to resist. It's confession time. I want you and I want you very badly!'

Far from frightening her, it filled her with joy, and her dark eyes searched his face, looking for the truth and finding it. She lifted her arms and linked them behind his neck as he bent to her again, but he removed them gently, placing them by her sides, pressing her deeply into the soft cushions as his lips trailed over her creamy face, the silken skin of her neck, his hands insistent as he shaped her body until her breath was no more than shallow gasps of delight, her arms too languid to lift.

His fingers pushed aside her dressing-gown, allowing his hand to trail down the deep valley between her breasts, the soft material of her nightdress hardly a barrier at all. He touched her neck gently, his eyes darkening as he noticed again the marks still livid against her skin.

'If I see him again, I'll probably kill him,' he murmured thickly, his mouth moving against her skin.

Tara was almost fainting with pleasure, unable to differentiate between dreams and reality, her small cries shocking even to her own ears. She had never felt like this before, never known complete desire, and Ben seemed to have lost all idea of reality too.

He pulled the ties that held her nightdress, moving it from her shoulders, his eyes intent on the thrusting beauty of her breasts, the hard, excited nipples inviting before his hungry gaze, but she was too involved to be shy. Whatever Ben wanted was what she wanted too.

'Oh, please, Ben!' she gasped, lifting her arms and pulling his head down to her, leaping with shocked delight as his mouth closed warmly over one throbbing breast, easing the taut pain.

'Dear God!' he gasped, his hands possessive and hard as he caught her violently to him, his tongue making circles of fire around the tender, aching peak, and she slid her fingers into his thick, dark hair, cradling him against her before he lifted his head, searching hungrily for her lips, his hand possessively covering the swollen beauty of her breast.

'Have you ever felt like this before?' he muttered. 'Does Lambourne make you feel like this? How often have you slept with him?'

It was like a slap, a shower of cold water, and she cringed away from him, from the hostile intensity of his golden eyes.

'I've never slept with anyone!' she said tremulously. 'Nobody has ever even seen me, nobody but you!' She knew that by saying that she was putting herself completely at his mercy, but there was nothing else to say, and deep inside she was prepared for the shudder of rejection that seemed actually to shake his powerful body.

For a second, he looked at her as if he had never seen her before, his eyes searching her face, and then his whole expression changed and he was back to normal, Ben Shapiro, clever, hard, filled with angry sarcasm.

He lifted himself away from her, his eyes flaring over her before he steadily fastened her nightdress and the buttons of her dressing-gown.

'Too bad, kitten,' he said ironically. 'Help I will, teach I will not!'

He helped her to her feet, not relenting even when he saw her stricken face, but catching her as she swayed dizzily.

'I want you,' he assured her quietly, 'but you're just too easy to take. Tomorrow we make other arrangements.'

Suddenly he was gone and Tara ran to her room, locking the door and falling into bed, the covers pulled over her to smother the storm of weeping.

*   *   *

In the morning, the first thing she saw as she came out of her room was a suitcase, Ben's, and he looked up as she came into the kitchen, his eyes noting the remaining signs of distress on her face.

'I'm moving out,' he said quietly. 'I'll take my things as I go into the office, and then you can have the flat to yourself. I'll give you my keys.'

'Don't bother,' said Tara in a low voice, her eyes on her tightly clasped hands. 'I should never have been here in the first place and I'm the one who is moving out. In any case, I told you yesterday that I intended to book into an hotel this morning.'

'No.' He was instantly aggressive. 'I'm not the one in danger. Until we get this thing with Lambourne sorted to my satisfaction, I want you to stay here.'

'It's already sorted to my satisfaction,' said Tara firmly, looking up into his angry face. 'Whatever arrangements you make I shall not keep to them, so you may as well know it. This is your flat. I'm staying at an hotel until Mirry is out and walking.'

For a second she thought that he was about to come around the table and shake her as angrily as Martin had done, but he seemed to keep his temper by a great effort. He picked up his jacket, tossed the keys of the flat on to the table and walked out, taking his suitcase and abandoning his breakfast.

Tara waited no longer. The night before she had wept, but she had thought too, and she was not one to let the grass grow beneath her. Within minutes of his leaving she had found an envelope and placed the keys in it, packed her things and called a taxi. For now at least, a game of hide and seek was in progress, and at the end of it she would have made her break from IST.

The taxi waited until she had darted into the main office building and left the keys at the desk for Ben, with a message that they were to be handed straight to him. Then she was on her way, looking for an hotel at the other side of town, a corner to run to until these wounds were healed.

For the rest of the day she hunted for jobs, calling to see her mother at a time when she knew that Ben would be too busy to be there. She had every intention of varying her times, too. There was no way that she was going to be trapped at the hospital and coerced into anything. IST owed her some holiday, and she was taking it. If he fired her, then so much the better.

She had more success than she had dreamed possible during the next few days, three firms offering her a job straight off, subject to references. That was the stumbling block, of course. They had said it with a smile, her reputation being so good in her field, and she supposed there was just the uneasy doubt in their minds as to why she was leaving IST. Her story about a job with less travel didn't ring altogether true, but she would have to face Ben sooner or later, and there were also plenty of other people who would be willing to speak for her.

Her last interview towards the end of the week kept her later than she had thought, and she had to race to the hospital to get there at a safe time. It was tricky, too, to deceive Mirry. Her mother was not at all easy to deceive, indeed she had never had to face this situation before in her life, and she was aware that her face would have given her away if her mother had been at all her normal self.

As it was, she got away with it. Ben, it appeared,

had visited every day, like Tara at different times, and she felt a cold shiver as she realised that he was in fact looking for her. She had expected nothing else, after all.

It was the day that her luck ran out. As she was leaving the hospital he was just arriving, and he grabbed her arm as if he had captured a criminal.

'Where the hell have you been?' he rasped. 'I rang the flat as soon as I got to the office and you were already out of there! Do you realise that I've been searching the whole town for you? Had it not been for the fact that you were coming to see Miriam I would have had no idea whether you were alive or dead!'

'I told you that I had no intention of staying at the flat,' Tara said coolly. 'I left the keys at reception, so I can't think why you thought it necessary to ring the flat.'

'I rang immediately, before I got the keys. I wanted to talk to you to explain about . . .'

'There's nothing to explain,' Tara said as coldly as she could. 'I may as well tell you that I'm not coming back to IST. You can count this week and next as my resignation time. You require a month's notice. I'm therefore giving you two weeks, and as to the other two—sue me!'

She walked off on trembling legs, devastated when he did not pursue her. He knew it was for the best, apparently. The situation now was untenable. Naturally he knew that she could not work there with him again. She told herself that it was only sensible, that she would think up some explanation to give to Mirry—break it to her gently. As yet she had no idea what that explanation would be, but somehow it

would be all right. It would have to be. She had got
over worse things, after all.

By Monday she felt that she had to go in to the
office. She had to get the rest of her things out of there
and face Ben for the last time. Then she would start
moving them from the lodge, a *fait accompli* before
Mirry was out of hospital. In any case, she could not
go on paying hotel bills. She had decided that every
penny they had would be spent on the hospital fees.
After all, there had been insurance. Quite a bit of it
was gone, but there was a lot left.

It was odd to think that nobody at IST knew a thing
about her change of plans. They all wanted to know
about her mother. Martin and his outburst were not
mentioned. She cleared her desk with a certain
amount of stealth and then straightened up
determinedly to face Ben.

Joan beamed on her and chattered on when all Tara
wanted to do was get in to Ben's office and get it all
over with, but at last she was told to go straight in.
She had heard that one before. She knocked very
loudly indeed, only going in when Ben called out
impatiently for her to enter.

This time he was alone, standing by his desk
looking startled. Even so, she glanced round rapidly
as if she expected to find Wanda hidden behind the
door.

'Is it necessary almost to break the door down?' he
asked mockingly. 'The handle seemed to work fairly
well ten minutes ago. Nobody under the desk,' he
added derisively as he watched her stealthy glances
roam quickly around. 'There is, of course, the
cupboard, but as it's almost all shelves, I've always

found it difficult to bundle women in there.'

'I've come to resign officially,' Tara said coldly, her cheeks flushing at his mocking tone. 'Before I leave the building I'll have it typed out and left with you. I've been offered a job with Gregson's and I'm taking it.'

'A stuffy sort of firm,' he confided softly. 'They'll never get used to your fighting ways. You'll not last a week.'

'I'll change my image with no trouble at all,' said Tara tightly. 'In any case, it doesn't concern IST. I only came to tell you personally so that you . . .'

'Wouldn't think you were scared to face me?' he suggested mockingly. 'I would never have thought that! I know you have nerve enough for any occasion. In any case, surely your new post was offered subject to references being suitable? At least, that's what they said in their letter to me.'

'And you refuse to give me a reference?' Tara said scathingly. She might have known that he would already be in the picture. 'I would have thought you above that sort of thing, especially in the circumstances.'

'Oh, I am! Thank you for the thought,' he murmured quietly, his eyes brilliantly on her. 'There's a space, though, for reasons why you're leaving here. That's a bit tricky. I can hardly say unsuitable. Everybody in town knows your value to IST. So what do I say? That I refused to make love to you and you're hurting badly?'

'I'm not hurting at all,' Tara snapped, her face going pale. 'You can put down that I refuse to be sexually harassed, and that two members of this firm find that impossible to swallow.'

'Oh, one is very contrite!' he said tautly, his mouth losing its mocking smile. 'The other is in Brazil.'

'You risked sending him back?' Tara was so much a part of this firm that she forgot her own problems entirely for a few seconds and he noticed, his eyes losing some of the bleak look.

'It wasn't too difficult to work out,' he said quietly. 'Dismissed and hanging around town he could have got into all manner of trouble, including searching for you. In Brazil, he's powerless and he'll have time to come to his senses. They do say that these brilliant people are easy to upset.'

Brilliant! Ben was the most brilliant person here and he was steady as a rock!

'What about the firm?' she asked a little anxiously. 'Suppose that . . .'

'I have a close friend right on the spot,' he assured her. 'One step out of line, one tiny bit of sabotage and Lambourne's fired at once and stranded in Brazil. I reckon he's getting a very good deal after all, and had it not been for his endangering you by being here he would have been out on his ear already,' he finished angrily.

'Well, if you're satisfied, I'll be going,' Tara said huskily, not wanting to hasten the moment when she would never see him again. She turned to the door but his voice, faintly mocking, again stopped her.

'There's a little matter of your contract,' he said softly. 'The terms are a month's notice on either side, subject to mutual agreement. I do not agree. I do not sell or give away the family silver, as I told you before. You're precious to the firm, the ace up my sleeve. I refuse to part with you.'

'Unless you propose to bundle me into that cupboard and lock the door, then I fail to see how you can stop me from breaking my contract and telling Gregson's exactly what I like about your refusal to give me a reference.'

Tara turned away again, but he still held all the aces.

'We had another bargain, Miss Frost!' he said silkily. 'I wanted to pay for Miriam's operation. *You* insisted upon paying yourself.' He opened the desk drawer and tossed a paper towards her. It skidded to the edge of the desk and she walked back rather fearfully to look. She thought she had enough, but even so her heart began to take on an unnatural beat. It leapt right into her throat at the amount she saw.

'Of course, that's only a preliminary account, you understand?' he said quietly. 'Normally the accounts go out at the end of the month, but after our little chat at the hospital I knew you would want some idea fairly soon. So far they've come up with this. The final amount will come about a month after Miriam has left hospital.'

She just stared at it horrified, longing to sit down, but he did not invite her to sit, he did not even sit himself. He had been standing since she came into the room, making everything look small.

'I would think, by the look on your face, that this amount outpaces your savings,' he said softly. 'Of course, there's absolutely no need to worry. I'm still willing to pay it all.'

'No!' Tara looked up at him anxiously. 'I'll pay what we've got, and then I'll still do the job you want, if that's what you insist on.'

'But of course it is,' he said with a look of exaggerated surprise at her. 'It was part of the arrangement.'

'Then I'll give you my address and when you need—need a hostess, I'll arrange to be there. You can leave a message at Gregson's and . . .'

'But my dear Miss Frost,' he said reasonably, 'I thought that I made myself quite clear. You're an asset to the firm and an asset to me only while you are part of the firm. Who would take a tiny little thing like you seriously once you were parted from IST? And think of the speculation the arrangement would then fire! No, things stand as agreed. You stay here on the staff and this is an extra job to earn much-needed cash. When we're all nicely squared up, then come to me again and say that you're leaving.'

'You always win, don't you?' Tara said angrily, tears in her eyes that were only partly rage. 'You're always one jump ahead.'

'I try to be,' he said, softly mocking, 'and I have been known to have some small success. As you're staying in town to be near Miriam, and as your days will now be free since there will be no need to race around looking for a job, I expect you back at your desk tomorrow morning bright and early. IST is missing your boundless energy.'

There was nothing left to do but turn and walk out, utterly defeated. But he had not finished.

'Tara,' he said quietly, his eyes skimming over her as she turned to face him accusingly, 'it's time to start eating again. By the look of you, one of the firm's assets is dwindling. We don't want you to look half starved and ill when you stand by me to welcome guests at Ellerdale Manor, do we?'

At any other time, he would have never got away with that, but right now Tara had had more than enough. She simply walked out, ignoring the look in his eyes, hating herself for finding out that her guardian angel had a heart of stone, after all.

CHAPTER NINE

IT WOULD go down as the worst week of her life, Tara decided, after a full five days back at IST. She felt so different, behaved so differently, that she hardly knew herself. Love was supposed to fill you with joy, boundless energy. It had drained her reserves until she was barely attached to the earth. The bi-weekly meetings that were part of the office organisation were a small, much-dreaded nightmare, her comments only made when necessary, her voice so low that she felt herself to be mumbling, her eyes rarely leaving either her notes or her clenched hands.

Ben was not pleased. According to Joan he was very difficult to please nowadays, a subject for constant complaint whenever she came into contact with Tara, and certainly he seemed to be staying in his office almost all the time, his days of wandering around keeping in close touch with events apparently over. Gone were the times when she would look up to find him entering her office or chatting to some member of staff outside her door.

He did not visit her mother either, although twice during the week he had sent flowers. The only bright spot was that Mirry was progressing well, the daily physiotherapy bringing life back to her once useless limbs and a great deal of pleasure to her face.

She had no idea that this was costing a fortune. Naturally she knew that she was in a private room, and they were well able to afford that. It had been the subject of their discussion before she went into hospital. What she did not know, had not yet apparently discovered, was that everything else was private too. The account that Tara had seen so briefly had contained a whole list of expenses ranging from X-rays, to path. lab., to the anaesthetist, and finally the surgeon himself. Tara felt herself to be almost as unworldly as her mother that she had not known the approximate cost of such things, but it would have made little difference. The operation had had to be done and done fast before Mirry's nerve had run out.

She was well aware that Ben still wanted to pay, in spite of their personal feud. He had used it merely to keep her in the firm, but his ruthlessness had startled her, although why it should have she could not think. He was after all a hard-headed businessman, though why he found her so irreplaceable, considering her nuisance value, she could not imagine.

For a whole week he left her severely alone, but in the middle of the following week she was summoned to his ofice. He was not at all friendly either, the amused irony now gone completely from his eyes, the warm topaz now a cool gold.

'Sit down, Tara,' he said quietly, indicating the chair opposite his desk. 'Something has come up which may well please you, and as you're going to be involved we should discuss it now.'

At the moment she could not think of one thing to please her, but she tried to look businesslike and after one sharp glance at her he continued, 'The function we went to where you were speaking to Patrick Ndele, you remember?'

She did! It seemed to have been the beginning of the end. She just nodded and he went on, 'You spoke to Ndele about the flooding in Omari, and I spent the better part of the evening working my way around other people, drumming up support too.'

She began to look interested and he leaned back in his chair, his eyes on her face. 'There is to be a fund set up and I've been asked to organise the whole thing. It's being launched at a charity gala this week. Quite a few celebrities have promised to be there, at least two pop groups, two or three actors and so on. I want you to be there with me.'

'All right!' For the first time she was nervous about attending such a function, but she would not let Ben see that.

'I will have to start the proceedings with a few words, and I think it would be nice if you said something too. You were out there right at the beginning and you could tell them about . . .'

'No! Oh, please, no!' Tara was on her feet at once and he looked genuinely surprised. 'I couldn't! All those people! I—I'll go with you but . . .'

'You thrive on such things,' he reminded her in a startled voice. 'It's been part of your job since you came here. The only difference will be that this time you'll not be putting the firm across in a good light, you'll be making people see the necessity for action. It's something you believe in.'

'I know! But I can't stand up there and . . . I don't feel able to any more, somehow. I—I seem to have lost my nerve for—things,' she finished in a low voice, avoiding his eyes and sinking back to her seat.

He swore softly under his breath, but when she

looked up a trifle fearfully he was just looking at her intently.

'Right,' he said briskly. 'I'll do the talking, you just be there and—glitter a little.'

She didn't feel she had much of that either, but she had got away with this one and she was not about to push her luck. She nodded and made thankfully for the door when they had discussed times and places. His voice stopped her as she had her hand on the handle.

'We'll call it an extra job,' he said with quiet cruelty. 'I'll give you a cheque later.'

Tara walked out before he could see her face. She had once told herself that you didn't really know a person at all. Clearly she had been right.

It wasn't much of a nightmare. After seeing the colossal bill from the hospital, Tara had decided that she could no longer afford hotels and had moved back to their old flat, which was now only partly furnished and quite cheerless. She went quickly out when Ben called for her on the evening in question, determined that he was not going to see how frugally she was living, but he had made no move even to get out of the car until he saw her.

She sat with her hands clenched in her lap, a habit that was growing, and reminded herself that she had wanted him to stay out of her life, stop wading in where he was not wanted. He had now taken it all to heart and she was lonely, lonelier than she would ever have thought possible.

He said nothing either on the way and made no attempt to raise her flagging spirits. She was at last the dead weight she had once threatened to be, silent and scared, not at all herself, but he seemed not even to notice.

It was like the first night of a film première. The foyer was glittering with extra lights, television cameras were set up both inside and outside the building, as people waited to get a glimpse of the stars who had promised their services, and Tara clung to Ben's arm, her grip tightening to panic level when he was stopped to say a few words to viewers at home.

He was smooth, she admitted, no more put out than he would have been at a meeting in the office, and as the cameras turned to her he politely led her away, pointedly not hearing any further requests. She had a choking sense of gratitude that grew as he escorted her into the room and settled her quietly in her seat at the main table as if she were just somebody he had brought for an evening out.

Tara would not have believed that she could have got like this in so short a time. She was almost too scared to breathe, wanting to run from there. If this was what love did . . . She relaxed but slowly as the evening progressed. Their table was raised slightly, Ben in the seat of honour, Tara at his side, and at first she had felt herself to be the object of all eyes, but this passed off as things got under way. The place was packed. Tables for six all around the room, filled completely, many faces that she knew from television, and as the performances began she almost began to enjoy herself, although Ben was coolly polite and no more than that.

It was during a break half-way through the proceedings that Ben was supposed to make his appeal and launch the fund, and once again all eyes turned in their direction. Tara's heart returned to her mouth too in case his new-found cruelty surfaced and he called on her to speak.

He was witty and cunning, she decided. He had the audience spellbound and it was only at the end that he looked down at her and frightened her.

'All of you here will have seen at some time the devastation that any kind of flooding can cause,' he said. 'From time to time, watery disaster strikes at the innocent and we see the pictures that are flashed across the world and appear on our television screens. Only a few of you will have seen the results at first hand. My partner tonight is Tara Frost of IST. She was in Omari when things were very bad, before help in any reasonable form reached the people. She has been partly responsible for this appeal.' He looked down at her and smiled. 'She is not going to give any kind of speech, but I'm sure that she will be only too pleased to speak to anyone who wants to know more after we have finished.'

Tara gave an audible sigh of relief as he sat down, turning to him to thank him, but he was not even looking in her direction and her eyes were startled as a voice rose when the applause finished.

'*Vive la belle Tara!* Speech! Speech!'

She stared in amazement at the tall, good-looking man who had come to his feet, several grinning companions with him, and her smile grew as she recognised Pierre Lepage, the French doctor from Omari, there with some of the medical team whose good humour had made life almost agreeable out there. Ben covered her hand with his, half rising, suddenly protective again, but her fear was not so great that she could not meet this challenge.

'Ladies and gentlemen,' she said, rising only for a moment, 'Mr Shapiro talked of first-hand knowledge. The first people on the scene were a French medical team. For many days, they alone answered the cry for help. They worked in dreadful conditions with little equipment and almost no sleep. I think another speech would be a very good idea, but not from me. Ladies and gentlemen, Dr Pierre Lepage!' She gave a small bow towards him and he looked quite taken aback but rose to his feet, his laughing eyes admiring the neat twist of events, and soon he had the audience as spellbound as Ben had done.

'Well fielded and beautifully passed,' Ben said softly, the protective hand now removed, and Tara wondered how she had managed to summon up that little burst of confidence.

She stole a look at Ben's face. It was coldly handsome, his eyes on the person who leaned across to whisper to him, and then he gave full attention to the Frenchman, his expression quite impassive. He seemed to have forgotten that she was here. Tara wished that she could forget him as readily.

As she left, the whole French group lined up to waylay her and she felt quite surprised to see how handsome Pierre Lepage was. In the dirt and turmoil of Omari he had been merely a good-humoured doctor with nothing on his mind but the work in hand. Here, she saw him as a man for the first time.

'I knew that there was great beauty somewhere under the hot and mud-streaked image I saw every day in Omari,' he said with an admiring look at her. 'You are very quick to retaliate, Tara! I came merely to observe and hope for help for those people. I did not expect to be pushed into the front of things, especially by one so small and delicate. I think that you owe me a favour.'

'I will say with caution, name it!' Tara laughed.

Ben had been called from her side for a moment and Pierre looked across at him quizzically.

'That is the man who came to shout at you, is it not? He is your employer only?' His quick eyes noted her blushes, the sudden tightening of her lips. 'He will not attack me if I invite you to dinner? I ask this because he is not a weak-looking man, and I remember well his rage.'

'I work for him, nothing more,' Tara said as easily as she could, smiling at his amused words. 'I'd love to have dinner with you, Pierre. Just name the time and the place.'

They were still making arrangements when Ben came back to collect her, his smile at the French party tight and cold.

'Going out with Lepage?' he asked briefly as they were driving back.

'Yes.' Tara took a minute to decide whether or not to tell him to mind his own business, but thought better of it. 'Dinner tomorrow night.'

'Remember that the French expect value for money,' he said sardonically. 'Maybe you should take some of the ointment along.'

Tara didn't deign to answer, and as they drew up at her flat she simply got out and walked off. After all, she had nothing to thank him for.

As she got ready for bed, she felt numb with misery. The one flare of her old self had reminded her bitterly

of all that Ben Shapiro had taken from her. Her
instincts had been good, she had been right to try to
exclude him from her life, he just had not allowed her
to do it. Even now, his reasons were a puzzle. It would
have been good to be able to compare notes with
anyone else he had helped, to see if he had also left
their lives empty and unhappy. Everyone at work
looked happy enough to her, except herself—and Ben.

The knock on the door was just the last straw. If
Janet had come round to commiserate with her at this
late hour then she would just have to be told to go.
The fact that she was ready for bed would be excuse
enough. She opened the door wearily and almost
jumped out of her skin at the sight of Ben standing
there, grim-faced.

'Do you normally open the door to any Tom, Dick
or Harry?' he asked irascibly, walking in uninvited.

'I don't know any of them,' Tara said sarcastically,
'and I imagined it was Janet. What do you want?'

'God knows!'

He was prowling around like a bad-tempered bear,
his eyes taking in the scarcity of furnishings.

'What the hell are you living here for, anyway?' he
suddenly ground out. 'It's almost empty. Couldn't
you find a decent hotel?'

'Plenty!' Tara said, taking her stand by the door and
waiting pointedly for him to leave. 'Fortunately, I can
live here rent free, being part owner. If you would just
tell me why you're here, perhaps we can get it over
with and I can get to bed.'

He stopped prowling, standing in the middle of the
floor and looking at her almost violently. It made her
uncomfortably aware of her state of dress. Night attire

was not the sort of thing she would have preferred to be in at this time.

'Why didn't you stay at my flat?' he rasped angrily. 'I wouldn't have bothered you. You know me better than that.'

'I didn't wish to stay at your flat,' Tara snapped. 'And I don't know you at all.'

'Why won't you let me look after you while Miriam is in hospital?' he insisted, ignoring everything else. 'I have no idea from one day to the next what you're doing.'

'Why should you have?' Tara cried exasperatedly. 'Go and ask Joan what she's doing! Why pick on me? If you want to take care of Mirry, then go ahead and do it, visit her, sit by her, hold her hand. I am neither sick nor incompetent. I don't need a watch-dog.'

'What are you doing now?' he asked irritably, glaring at her clothes, her bare feet. 'Practising for after-dinner drinks tomorrow?'

Her temper flared over the top.

'Out!' she raged, opening the door and standing back. 'When I want to be insulted I'll give you a quick call, but don't hold your breath!'

He strode to the door and slammed it, turning to grab her arms and hold her fast.

'Listen to me, you irritating little . . .' he began furiously. His voice trailed away as she glared up at him, her tilted eyes wide and furious, and he suddenly began to laugh softly.

'Oh, what the hell,' he murmured tauntingly. 'It's a well-known fact that you can't train a kitten!'

He pulled her to him, capturing her startled lips, his hands holding her head to his as he kissed her with apparent satisfaction, his lips lingering until she was thoroughly subdued.

'Keep that in mind!' he said in a self-satisfied manner as he lifted his head, his hands firm and sure on her slender hips. 'Remember that Frenchmen are not at all to be trusted!'

He opened the door, leaving her shaking and almost open-mouthed, turning as he left to toss in one of his usual sardonic comments.

'And wear more than that when you bring him back here tomorrow night! See that you eat plenty at dinner too—you're all eyes and brittle bones.'

There was nothing at hand to throw, and in any case he was gone before she could gather herself together and ask herself exactly what had happened there. It could hardly be called protective behaviour. He had probably come to apologise for his rudeness earlier, she decided. Of course, his normal character had surfaced as soon as she had opened her mouth. It was funny, though, she no longer felt lifeless and weary. He had a way of sparking her into irritated life.

It seemed to have sparked him into life, too, because he was in her office first thing next morning looking very pleased with himself.

'Call off the dogs!' he murmured as he saw her tight and wary expression. 'I came to tell you that the fund is started and already with the takings last night and promises of money plus cheques to date we have over a hundred and fifty thousand!'

'Pounds?' Tara gasped.

'Pounds,' he laughed. 'As soon as I appeared on TV, it seems that every firm in the city was falling over itself to make a huge donation!'

'Professional jealousy,' Tara said smugly, and he nodded delightedly.

'I had hoped to find that. Nobody wants to be left out. Come and give us a hand, leave everything else. Joan and I are snowed under.'

'You're doing it from here?' Tara asked astonished.

'Of course!' he said with a laugh. 'It cuts costs. I want every penny out in Omari, and I know just the person to see that it reaches the people!'

'Me?' Tara said hopefully, standing and pushing all her own work to the side of her desk.

'Normally, yes,' he said quietly, his topaz eyes intent on her suddenly eager face. 'Things are not at all normal at the moment, though.'

He turned to go, expecting her to follow, but she held her ground.

'What's not normal?' she asked determinedly, and he turned back to look at her squarely.

'First of all, there's Miriam in hospital, then of course, I remember Omari and you're looking a bit frail lately.'

'I'm not!' Tara snapped irritably. 'I know what to expect. I can organise things from the capital,' she added, looking decidedly abashed as his dark brows rose quizzically.

'That last item apart,' he said softly, 'I've decided that you can't be the one and that's that. If you want to know the main reason, here it is. I need you!'

'What on earth for?' she asked irritably, following him along the passage.

'This and that,' he said silkily. 'In here, Tara, this is where it's all happening. One final word, I'm going to ask Lepage to go to Omari. Tell him tonight, will you? He can give me a ring.'

'Why Pierre?' Tara insisted with growing annoyance. 'You don't know him from Adam.'

'I'm used to making quick decisions,' he said with infuriating calm. 'Stop snapping at my heels, there's a good girl. Get a ledger from Joan and start making entries. For the moment, the work is all here!'

'I'll not ask Pierre!' Tara threatened, collecting the ledger that a very harassed Joan held out to her, and pulling a chair to the spare desk. Ben was in his own office, the door wide open.

'Get ready to be fired!' he called with no annoyance whatever in his voice.

It was fascinating to see the money columns grow. For the whole day the switchboard was ringing, routing calls to Joan, Ben and Tara. The business of IST came almost to a standstill as the fund grew and grew. They were all caught up with it, no moment to spare, and Tara forgot her own problems entirely.

'Let's do a grand total,' said Ben as the day drew to a close. Tara's hand had become cramped with writing in large sums of money and the names of the donating firms and individuals.

'Wait until I get this last one down,' she muttered, scribbling quickly. 'No wonder we made so much last night, the tickets were five hundred pounds each!'

'It wasn't a stingy do!' Ben said mockingly.

'I didn't pay anything!' Tara reminded him, looking up guiltily.

'You were with me,' he said softly, his eyes skimming her excited face. 'Who takes a beautiful girl out for the evening and expects her to pay her share? You must know some pretty odd people!'

Tara looked rapidly away, blushing wildly, and his strong hand reached out for the book.

'Now, let's see,' he said. 'It doesn't look at all bad for the first day.'

'It's furiously exciting,' Tara exclaimed, and his soft laughter sent shivers right through her.

'Going on for a quarter of a million!' he said after rapid and intent calculations as both Tara and Joan hovered over him. 'Not bad for a start!'

'Not bad? It's fantastic!' Tara protested excitedly. 'You're never satisfied!'

'Oh, I expect to be—finally!' he murmured quietly, his golden eyes flaring over her as he lifted his head.

'Well, there's a whole week to go yet!' Joan put in stoically, and Ben's grin had Tara's face flooding with colour at this utter naïveté on the part of his secretary.

She had to visit Mirry early because of her date with Pierre, and to her annoyance she found Ben already there when she arrived.

'I've just been telling Miriam that you have an exciting date tonight, Tara,' he said tauntingly as she bent to kiss her mother, who was now sitting in a chair in her room.

'Did you walk to this chair all by yourself?' Tara asked, ignoring Ben's remarks.

'Every step!' her mother said with pride. 'I'm getting along better every day. Today has seen a really big improvement. I've got a bit of news. If I do my exercises carefully and if I come back every other week, they're going to let me come home next weekend. Back to the lodge while this glorious weather lasts! I can hardly wait.'

'Back to the lodge?' Tara said in dismay. 'But Mirry, I thought we agreed that . . .'

'Oh, I know, dear,' her mother said soothingly. 'But Ben has pointed out that it won't take much to convert the place back to normal, and I love it there. I'll need it as it is for a few months yet, but after that Ben is going to get it turned back to a place for normal people, not invalids. He said that he'll never let anyone else have it, and if we go, he'll have it demolished. I couldn't bear it. I already think of it as home and when I can walk in that parkland . . .' She sighed happily. 'I want you to put the flat back into the hands of the agents, Tara,' she added briskly.

Her mother had never in her whole life shown this kind of determination, and Tara knew just exactly who was behind it all.

'You've talked her into that,' she said heatedly as Ben walked politely with her to the entrance as they left. 'You know what I had decided.'

'She loves the place,' he said with every sign of innocence, an innocence she did not believe at all. 'Surely we both want her to be happy?'

'You can stop this *both* business,' Tara snapped. 'I don't know what your motives are, but if it's so that I'll be tied to IST for ever and doing the hostess bit until I'm too old to stand, then forget it. Now that the flat is going back on the market I'll be able to pay that bill with no help at all. Get yourself a new hostess, Mr Shapiro!'

He stood there laughing as she stormed off, but she could already see possibilities of escape from this domination. He who laughs last, she thought grimly, her temper only just restored as she went out to meet

Pierre.

She had a lovely time, though. Somehow, her latest brushes with Ben had returned her to normal. She was not brooding any more, walking around lifelessly. She had half expected to find the whole French team there, but Pierre was adamant about that.

'Oh, they wanted to be, do not imagine otherwise,' he said with a laugh. 'However, I do not share my date and I asked you first.'

'Speaking of asking,' Tara said much against her better judgement, 'Ben wants to see you, if you could ring him tomorrow.'

'Ben? Ah! Your angry boss,' he said with sudden understanding. 'He is not about to take me to task for one date, surely? I will leave on the next flight to Paris.'

'No!' Tara laughed and found herself explaining the need to distribute the money swiftly with no red rape. Why she was doing this she did not know. She wanted to go out to Omari herself. Here she was, giving her job away.

He was very interested and suddenly sat up attentively.

'Why, here he is now!' he exclaimed. 'Perhaps we could join him and then I can discuss it right away.'

Tara had seen him too. She seemed to have developed antennae for knowing when he was near. He was not alone either, but this time it was not Wanda. This time it was a blonde, beautiful, and again clinging. They sat down and he was listening intently to her, his eyes never leaving her face. And she was beautiful, Tara admitted, her heart sinking. Another of his women. She turned back to Pierre.

'I think you'd better leave it for now,' she said
quietly. 'I don't think somehow he would like to be
disturbed when he has a date of that kind.'

'Perhaps not,' said Lepage, looking at her intently.
'She is certainly beautiful.' He reached across and
took her hand. 'You care for him, eh?'

'He's domineering, often irascible, taunting,
interfering—you saw how he was in Omari.'

'And you care for him very much,' he said softly.
'Does he rescue all his staff who are in uncomfortable
circumstances overseas?'

'I—well, I'm a little different,' Tara said in a
flustered voice. 'He cares a great deal for my mother.'

She had not realised that Pierre had such a loud
laugh. He simply erupted into sound, his handsome
head thrown back as he thoroughly enjoyed himself.
She felt like slamming her hand over his mouth, and
everyone seemed to be turning to look at them. Ben
would look too, she knew that; she had to pretend to
be amused but she could not wait to get outside.

Pierre, though, was disposed to linger. He
apologised profusely, but the grin remained and he
insisted that they sit back with coffee and brandy
while he talked a great deal. As much of it was very
amusing, Tara relaxed and decided not to spoil his
evening. Ben, it seemed, was anxious to leave, or
perhaps they had only come in for a small meal. At
any rate, they left just as Pierre finally called for the
bill and helped her to her feet.

They were still there as Tara came out with Pierre,
and he bowed pleasantly to Ben before walking to the
car with Tara. She had seen more than she wished to
see, though. Ben was putting his ladyfriend into a

taxi, and she flung her arms around him, kissing him repeatedly. As far as Tara could see, he did not object. The old pain flared up inside, no temper to help her, and she felt almost frantic with the need to escape from everyone.

Pierre's car was across the road and they were walking slowly towards a safe place to cross. Not quickly enough for her, and when she heard Ben's voice just behind her she panicked, unable to face him as she felt now.

'Tara.' He was right behind her without her even knowing it and, panic-stricken, she veered away from the sound of his voice, stepping out to cross the road, trying to outrun her shame and misery.

There was a frightening squeal of brakes and her senses returned as she looked in horror at the taxi that bore down on her. In that split second, she knew that it could never stop in time. Stupidly she had placed herself in this position by trying to outrun the man she would have run to for the rest of her life.

In that heartbeat of time, she gave up because there was no chance at all. The gleaming radiator seemed to fill her whole world, and then a tremendous force hit her, not from the taxi but from something else. The arm that collected her and almost threw her away from danger was the strongest in the world, she just knew that for sure. Her feet left the ground as the taxi stopped a few feet beyond where she had been standing a second before.

Everything swung wildly but she could see Ben's face, white and grim, furious as he held her tightly to him, crushing her and showing no sign of letting her go.

'Did I hit her? Is she all right, guv?' The taxi-driver jumped out, his passengers looking very shaken, the man himself looking slightly sick. 'I couldn't believe it! She just jumped under the old cab!'

'She's all right,' Ben said tersely, turning her head against his chest. 'She's just a bit shaken up. No fault of yours, you were fast on the brake. She's mine. It's my fault. She slipped the leash for a moment. I'll keep her under control in future. No harm done!'

Except to her whole life, to each day that would follow! The taxi-driver gave a sort of hysterical laugh at Ben's sardonic comments and the passers-by began to move off.

'Is she all right? Shall I have a look at her?' It was Pierre, all doctor, and Tara glanced at him and then closed her eyes.

'It didn't hit me,' she whispered.

'I'll see to her,' Ben said determinedly, his voice tight with anger. 'She just needs a damned good shaking and her brain will go back into the right slot!' He swung her up into his arms and strode off, ignoring astonished passers-by with a fine, regal indifference. 'Her brain works strangely. Sometimes it's easy, sometimes it drives you mad. She has this fantasy that she's indestructible!'

He breathed heavily as a dragon might breathe when the enemy was in sight, and Tara shivered against him, not daring to tell him that his arms were hurting, that he had probably cracked her ribs. She opened one eye cautiously and saw Pierre walking alongside, his grin widening when he saw her stealing a furtive look.

'Hold her while I get my car out!' Ben ordered

imperiously, handing her like child to Pierre. 'Don't
let her escape.'

He strode round the corner and Pierre let her feet
touch the ground as Tara opened her eyes, glancing
anxiously around.

'He's gone! It is safe to come out now!' Pierre was
laughing at her and Tara found her own lips
quivering in answering amusement. Ben was
terrifying in this sort of mood, and he had not finished
by any means.

'I was stupid . . .' Tara began.

'Do not worry, he knows that.' He looked closely at
her. 'You are truly all right?' he added with
professional concern. 'You had a very nasty shock,
even if the taxi did not hit you, and it appears that I
am about to be sent on my way. If you feel bad, you
had better tell me now before he comes roaring back.'

'No, I'm quite all right,' Tara assured him, keeping
quiet about the unexpected shaking that was going on
inside her, the desire to close her eyes and let the
world roll by. 'He'll want to take me home, I expect.'

'Naturally,' Pierre said with another wide grin. 'His
fondness for your mother would allow for nothing
less. I will telephone you tomorrow,' he added as
Ben's car came to a growling halt beside them. 'I
regret that the evening ended so badly.' He kissed her
hand and Ben was there at once, helping her into the
car, shaking hands with Pierre and driving off with all
speed.

CHAPTER TEN

'HOW do you feel?' Ben's voice was a tight sound in the darkness of the car, and Tara shuddered at the anger in him.

'I feel a bit shaken,' she confessed. 'I'll go straight to bed when I get home.'

'Hmm!' The angry growl was not at all encouraging. 'You'll pack an overnight bag and then you'll come with me.'

'We've been through all this before,' Tara began wearily, not wanting any argument now.

'Then let's go through it again!' he rasped. 'Listen very carefully. You will pack a bag and come with me. If you intend to put up any resistance, say so now because I'm quite prepared to turn around and take you to my flat without the comfort of any overnight bag. This little excursion is merely a kindness, knowing as I do the sheer necessity that women feel to have at least a hundredweight of small things about their person.'

His knowledge of women was no surprise, and she could hear the sheer determination in his voice.

'I'll come,' she said quietly. In any case, she was beginning to feel very shaken, light-headed and a trifle sick. The sight of the taxi kept looming up in her mind and she wanted to go to sleep with such a deep yearning that it astounded her.

In the flat she gathered her things very slowly and

172

then went to clean her face, knowing that as soon as she was at Ben's flat she would collapse.

'What's keeping you?' Ben's angry voice, threaded through with anxiety, was at the other side of the door.

'I'm washing my face,' she answered, and shrugged resignedly to herself when she heard his annoyed muttering. She was never going to live this down and she could only hope that he never suspected what it was that had driven her to such stupidity. Tears came to her eyes but she blinked them away irritably. It was no use crying for Ben. She would just have to be thankful that at least he cared about her enough to be worried when she was alone. Some people didn't even have that in their lives. She tried to count her blessings but gave up almost at once. She loved him. It was no use whatever.

In his flat it was dark, soothing and safe, and for a minute he said nothing at all, simply switching on the lights. The front door closed and there was silence, a large, uneasy silence that Tara dared not break.

'Go and get into bed,' he said quietly. 'I'll make you some sweet tea. It's supposed to be good for shock.'

She only wanted to sleep, to lay her head down and let sleep work its magic. She was not going to argue, though. She slid out of her dress and then, too weary suddenly to bother further, she climbed into bed in her half-slip and bra, sitting up with the sheets tightly round her as Ben came back in.

He handed her a cup of tea, so sweet that she felt quite revolted by it, but looking up at him from under her lashes she decided to suffer it.

'Are you all right?' It was an angry growl that

contained very little sympathy but a great deal of anxiety, and she nodded, keeping her eyes strictly on the cup in her hands.

'Y—yes, thank you. I'm just a little shaken.'

'Not as shaken as you ought to be.' He suddenly took the cup from her and placed it on the side-table, pulling her towards him, his hands tight on her bare arms.

'You were running away from me,' he accused wrathfully. 'You were so determined to get away from me that you almost killed yourself!'

He glared at her, tightening his grip until her face paled.

'I called to you! You heard me and you just stepped out under a taxi! Do I irritate you that much?'

'I didn't mean to do it, Ben! Surely you don't think that I . . .'

'I don't know what to think any more!' he grated, his topaz gaze angry and intent. His eyes roamed over her bare shoulders and then moved to the pallor of her face. 'Go to sleep,' he said gruffly. 'We'll talk tomorrow.'

'What do we have to talk about?' she asked unhappily, sliding down thankfully between the sheets, her eyes already closed.

'This and that,' he murmured quietly, his anger apparently lessening. 'How to keep you alive seems to be the priority at this moment.'

He went quietly out, closing the door but leaving the one lamp beside her bed still glowing, and her last thought was a ridiculous one. She had the distinct impression that he was going to stand guard over her while she slept. She would have been happier if he had stayed and held her instead, even if it had been only for a minute.

She could see the taxi! The driver was a fiend, aiming it at her, cutting her off when she tried to escape, and then it suddenly turned into a lorry, the noise of the engine like thunder as it slid across ice to loom over her. She could see her father and Mirry, and it would hit them too! She screamed but they didn't hear, even when she went on screaming as loudly as she could.

'Tara! Tara!' She opened terrified eyes to find Ben beside her, his hands hard on her shoulders, and her dazed eyes noticed the door wide open as if he had come in like a rocket. His hair was disordered, his robe tied loosely around him, and gradually, thankfully, she remembered where she was. It had been a dream, a nightmare.

'I—I could see the taxi, and the lorry that . . .' Tears filled her eyes and he lifted her up into his arms, his hand stroking her hair.

'Ssh!' he murmured in a shaken voice. 'You're safe now, quite safe. It's all over.'

For a minute he held her as she wept, his hands soothing and comforting until the present returned in full and the nightmare of the distant and nearer past faded away.

'I—I'm sorry,' she murmured, trying to move away, embarrassed that once again she had needed to have him there.

He let her move, but only far enough for his eyes to scan her face, and she had no idea what he saw there, but he threw back the covers and lifted her into his arms, cradling her to him.

'I'm all right!' she said anxiously, not finding it at all shocking to be here in his arms, only partly covered, the robe he wore open at the neck to show his brown chest and the covering of dark hair.

He did not answer. He simply walked to his room, kicking the door closed behind him, and slid her gently into the warmth of his bed, his hand smoothing her pale hair as he sat beside her and looked down at her.

'It's time you slept with somebody,' he said deeply. 'And of course, it can only be me.'

She stared at him for a second, her eyes wide and questioning, and he met her gaze seriously, his hand gentle against her face.

'I won't be one of your women, Ben,' she said tearfully, but he caught the hand that warded him off weakly and kissed her fingers one at a time.

'What women?' he asked softly. 'I've been too busy building a business to have a life overflowing with sensuous females. I'll be quite content with one, provided it's you.'

'What about that woman tonight?' she asked desperately. 'What about that glamorous woman who was kissing you outside the restaurant? I saw that and . . .'

'And you ran under a taxi!' he exclaimed, his face suddenly filled with understanding. 'Oh, Tara! Felice is my sister-in-law. And don't look like that,' he added quickly, 'if you begin to imagine that I'm having an affair with my sister-in-law I'll beat you!'

'She was kissing you!' Tara accused him. 'And in any case it doesn't make any difference because Wanda . . .'

'Let's deal with my affairs one at a time, shall we?' he said lazily, clearly not at all put out that she knew all about his women and hated them. 'Felice pounced on me this evening when I had something much more important to do. She's an actress—of sorts. Every play she's in seems to flop and I can't say that it surprises me. She spends a great deal of time trying to persuade me to back her in one way or another. Tonight she succeeded, to her astonishment, and the kisses were her extravagant way of showing her surprise.'

'You were talking intently at the table,' Tara said sharply, and he laughed, his eyes warmly on her angry face.

'Of course we were, sweetheart! I don't easily allow myself to be parted from thousands of pounds. I gave in only because I wanted to get rid of her. As I said, I had something important to do.'

'Why wasn't your brother there, then?' asked Tara triumphantly.

'My brother is a very smart chap,' he said seriously, his eyes filled with delight at her small battle. 'He lives overseas and Felice lives in England. If you don't believe me, we can telephone Abu Dhabi right now. He did think of joining the Foreign Legion, but a better offer came up.'

She watched him suspiciously and then said, 'Wanda is your—your . . . I saw you kissing her in your office.'

'She isn't and I was only kissing her because I heard you talking to Joan and I wanted you to be jealous. You were!' he ended smugly. 'It's been a great trial keeping Wanda around, waiting for those cat eyes to turn green. As soon as they did, I got rid of her—nicely, you understand.'

'It doesn't matter,' Tara said miserably. 'I don't have affairs and . . .'

'You and I, we love each other, don't we, kitten?' he said softly, lifting her up into his arms, and her dark eyes were filled with wonder as he brushed his lips across hers very gently. 'Don't we, darling?' he asked against her lips.

'Yes! Oh, yes!' she sobbed, clinging to him as his mouth opened over hers and he wrapped her in his arms.

He held her against him, his hands moving possessively over her. Minutes late he allowed her time to recover from the drugged feelings that his kisses had brought.

'You never did undress properly,' he murmured against her skin, his fingers unclipping her bra. 'I'm glad. I wanted to undress you myself.'

His hands moved with deep, caressing strokes that melted her until she seemed to be floating, her whole body in a state of warm surrender.

He slid the bra away, leaving his hands in warm possession of her swollen breasts, and her breathing changed to match his as his lips trailed down the length of her neck, stopping to brush her breasts and then moving in a ring of exotic caresses around her waist. He pushed her gently back to the soft pillows, leaning over her, not touching her at all except for his mouth against her shoulders, against the warmth of her skin, and then at the corner of her mouth as she turned her head desperately towards him.

When he gently removed the last skimpy coverings that hid her from him she was utterly molten, her eyes locked with his, closing in willing submission as his topaz gaze roamed over her.

'My little darling, you're so beautiful, so exquisite,' he murmured, huskily shaken. He bent his head and kissed the breasts that surged against him. 'Nothing will ever hurt you again,' he whispered.

She opened her eyes, her hands lifting lethargically to the dark head that bent over her, her fingers stroking through his hair, and he looked up at her slowly, the wonderful eyes half closed with desire.

'I want you,' he breathed. 'I love you!'

'Ben!' Her little cry of gladness brought his lips crushing down on hers, his hands to cup her face urgently as she opened up to him like a flower seeking the sun.

'I love you! I love you!' she gasped, tears flooding into her eyes but coming no further.

'I know, sweetheart! I know!' He shrugged out of his robe and came to her, gathering her to the hard power of his body. 'For a very long time, it has been inevitable.' He looked down at her, his eyes smiling, passion racing behind the golden gaze. 'There are stars in your eyes,' he said softly. 'May they always be there!'

'While you love me,' she said tremulously, sighing and arching to him as he moved over her, his lips on the silken skin of her neck.

'They're there forever, then,' he murmured thickly.

She seemed to be floating on a cloud as Ben caressed her, his hands moving with growing urgency over her body. And there was no shyness. There was nothing but ecstasy. She was drugged, in a trance-like state, completely pliant in his strong arms, her body moving against him at his subtle insistence. She was warm and slender, submissive, and his breathing became harsh and uneven as he touched her with growing passion.

'Tara!' Her soft sighs of pleasure seemed to be driving him mad. He could not stop now, he knew it. Her arms wrapped around him, her tongue teased the line of his jaw, and he gave a deep moan, his mouth buried against her shoulder as his hands claimed her breasts fiercely.

They seemed to swell beneath his touch, filling his hands, the peaks hard and demanding, and he gasped, almost in protest, his mouth moving with imperative necessity to each one in turn.

'Darling, I don't want to hurt you!' His voice was almost harsh with longing and she entwined her body with his, feeling the searing heat of his need as he responded violently to her action.

She cried out in fierce arousal as his mouth devoured her, his powerful body pressing her into the softness of the bed, his tongue exploring the sweet moisture of her mouth as his hands stroked over her.

'Honey!' he groaned. 'You're like sweet honey. I want to taste every part of you, make this last a whole lifetime.' His eyes were dark now, almost black with passion, the clear topaz drowned in the enlarged pupils. 'Am I driving you to this, darling? Do you want to make love with me?' The words were murmured hotly against her skin, and she gave a cry of happiness, clutching him to her. Even now in his great passion he was thinking of her, of her feelings, her needs.

'Don't leave me!' she gasped. 'Don't ever leave me!'
'Not even when I die,' he said harshly, his lips

unable to resist their tasting of her body.

His stroking hands found the secret core of her and she leapt in shock, colour flooding her face.

'Ben!' she moaned in protest, pleasure and shame mingled on her lovely face.

'Yes, darling! Yes!' he said demandingly, his lips hot against her own. 'You're mine, every part of you!' His body convulsed in an agony of arousal, and he pulled her fiercely to the hard cradle of his hips, his mouth silencing her moans of pleasure as he entered her with a powerful movement of his strong body.

White-hot pain and pleasure shot through her, making her tear her lips away to cry his name in a sharp, unearthly cry, and then her lips were captured again as he moved within her, taking her with a strange tenderness mixed with ferocity, a thrilling power that enslaved her for ever, reaching her soul.

'Tara!' His shuddering sigh was a sign of his own enslavement as waves of pleasure spiralled through them both and they drifted, spent and warm, through clouds of contentment, sensual delight still bringing shivers to Tara's slender body.

For moments they lay together, locked tightly in each other's arms, and then he raised his head, resting above her and looking down into her tilted eyes, searching the liquid darkness with a gleaming gaze that saw everything.

'My beautiful darling,' he murmured, breathing in the perfume of her skin. 'You didn't have a lot of choice, did you?'

There was rueful amusement in the deep, warm voice and she closed her eyes as he caressed her flushed face.

'I've never had a much of a choice since I met you,' she said softly, her lips touched with a smile.

'No,' he agreed quietly. 'I meant to have you, but you've fought me all the way.'

'Until now,' she reminded him blushingly, and he captured her mouth in a fierce kiss of pleasure.

'Until now,' he agreed in a satisfied voice. He moved to the side, taking her with him, enclosing her fast in his arms. 'When I first saw you,' he said softly, 'you delighted me. I thought I had never seen such an exquisite, unusual creature. I couldn't take my eyes off you. You were so clever, so full of determination and drive, but I think that even if you hadn't fitted into my team, I would have kept you there, made a job for you somehow. I used to saunter along past your office to have a look at you. I suppose for a whole month I never stopped smiling.'

He turned his head to capture her lips, turning her towards him.

'I can't stop looking at you now,' he complained with a laugh. 'You seemed to like me too,' he added ruefully, 'but I never imagined how I really felt until that dreadful evening of the accident. When I saw your face, all the life drained from it, the bewildered hurt, I knew that nothing again must hurt you. I knew why I wanted you close each day.'

'You took over my life,' said Tara with a loving look at him, ashamed that she had not understood.

'You drove me out of it!' he complained huskily. 'And suddenly, you hated me!'

'You scared me,' she protested. 'I felt swamped, taken over. I didn't understand. I was used to making my own way in the world and I enjoyed it. I didn't want to be taken over. I suspected you but I didn't know what I suspected. I didn't like it that I felt a bit lost without you!'

'Only a bit?' he asked with mocking sadness.

'Completely lost recently,' she confessed, her arms moving around his neck. 'I knew about the women and I knew that they meant nothing to you because of—of your wife.'

He looked at her sharply and then grimaced at what he saw, pulling her tightly to him, her head to his shoulder.

'I met Debra at university,' he said softly. 'We had an affair, my first. It seemed to be important that we marry, although neither of us felt much like it by the time we got around to it.' He sighed, his gaze on the ceiling, his mind obviously in the past. 'It was a mistake and it didn't last long. I was working like mad and Debra had met someone else. They wanted to marry and we had a very amicable divorce. We were always friends,' he added softly. 'That's why she felt able to come to me, and thank God she did. Before the marriage, her illness was diagnosed, and he didn't want to marry her. She came to tell me and the rest you know. I told you that I converted the lodge for my wife. Debra was no longer that but she was my friend right to the last, and I don't regret the time I spent trying to make her final days happy.'

He suddenly turned his head and looked down at her.

'Kitten! You're crying!' he said in a shocked voice, his arms tightening protectively.

'It doesn't matter,' she wept, her smile shining through the tears. 'I always had this feeling that you

were my guardian angel. I don't mind sharing that
with Debra!'

He lifted her on top of him, cupping her face and
looking into her eyes.

'Beautiful idiot!' he said thickly. 'I never felt less
like an angel. That's not what I want to be with you. I
want to be your lover, your husband, the one who is
always beside you, the one who wakes up with his
arms around you. It's the only heaven that I need.'

'You said—that night you said that you didn't teach.
You left me . . .'

'I left you hurting, I know,' he said regretfully. 'I
suppose I was over-protective then. I wanted you, led
you on, and then when I found out that I would be the
first I couldn't take such a sweet gift when you were
so in need of my help, when you weren't even
recovered from Lambourne's madness. I loved you
too much.'

'Does that mean you changed your mind tonight?'
Tara asked, trailing her lips against his skin.

'I nearly lost you,' he said tightly, his arms crushing
her. 'It changes the priorities. I had to have you close
enough to keep you safe. Only this is close enough!'

'You saved my life,' she said softly.

'And what use would mine be without you?' he
asked deeply. 'I love you, will always love you.'

He held her tightly, neither of them speaking, their
breathing as one, and then she said, worriedly, 'Were
you and Wanda . . . was she . . .?'

'No!' he said fiercely. He lifted his hand lazily and
trailed it across her breasts. 'I was too busy trying to
work out how to get you, and I had problems, Martin
being but one of them, you being the greatest. Mind

you, I had a certain amount of help from Miriam, at least she liked me!'

'I was jealous,' Tara confessed tremulously, and he pulled her more closely to him still, stroking her face.

'I'll never let you go,' he said softly. 'I'll never let you out of my sight again. We'll live at the manor. You love it, don't you?'

'Yes!' She smiled into his eyes, seeing them darken again as his fingers flexed against her skin.

'More than me?' he teased quietly, sensual pleasure in his intent gaze.

'Nothing more than you,' she said, her own smile dying as tiny flames seemed to lick over her, drawing her shuddering towards him.

'I want to make love to you again,' he confessed ruefully, 'but I'm not sure if it would be good for you. You had a bad shock this evening.'

'I'm all right now,' said Tara winsomely, looking up into his face as he moved her back to the softness of the bed.

'Shameless girl!' he said softly. 'I'll be too tired to go to the office tomorrow. You can stay here and play house!'

'I'm going to work!' said Tara determinedly, and his eyes narrowed on her face.

'Still the career woman?'

'If I stay here, I'll not see you until you get back,' she confessed, blushing under his intent gaze.

'Then you can get up and go to work,' he said happily. 'You can work in my office, we'll lock Joan out!'

He looked down at her with love and desire on his face. 'Are you going to marry me, darling?' he asked softly.

'Yes!' she cried, throwing her arms around his neck.

'One week!' he said decisively, grinning when she leaned back and gasped.

'It's not possible! I couldn't . . . What about Mirry?'

'We'll get her out for the event. She did say that she could leave this weekend. I'll speak to Burgess tomorrow. Today,' he corrected, looking at his watch.

Tara smiled, willing to drown in the kisses he rained on her then, and finally she managed to ask the question her mind had suddenly thrown out.

'How did you manage to be at that restaurant tonight?'

'I was following you, of course,' he said arrogantly. 'I heard the arrangement you made with Lepage.'

'But you said that you had something to do that was important, that's why you agreed to back Felice.'

'I did have something to do,' he assured her sternly. 'I had to follow you and that Frenchman back to your flat and sit outside to see if the lights went out. If they had done, I would have broken the door down and strangled him.'

'He was a bit scared of you,' Tara told him, laughing up into his possessive face.

'So what was he roaring with laughter about?' he asked suspiciously.

'I—I told him that you looked after me because—because you were fond of my mother,' Tara confessed with a wild blush, a blush that deepened at Ben's amused grin.

'Oh, I am,' he said softly, 'but I'm wild about her daughter. I told you I was good at making quick judgements,' he added. 'Lepage will do the job I have in mind very nicely. His speedy departure tonight shows his good taste.'

'It wasn't that,' Tara protested. 'He was scared of you!'

'That's good taste, too. You're mine! Anyone else can just stand well clear!'

She covered his face with tiny heated kisses until he groaned in protest, pulling her tightly against him.

'We should go to sleep,' he said. 'I'm supposed to be looking after you. A few more seconds and neither of us will be at work tomorrow.'

She bit her lip, secretly, her wide eyes looking longingly into his, and he took her hand, raising it to his lips.

'You're tempting me, kitten!' he murmured softly. 'Just remember you're indispensable to the firm. Tomorrow you'll need to be full of that energy.'

'It's all come back,' she told him, holding tightly to the hand that held hers. 'Ever since I knew that you loved me I've felt filled with energy.'

His golden gaze flared possessively over her.

'Then you won't need much sleep,' he said seductively, his lips moving over her face. 'Maybe we'll both stay at home and play house tomorrow, and the next day and the next . . .'

Tara closed her eyes, her body restless against his, her arms around him, and all worries faded. She needed no guardian angel. Heaven was wherever Ben was, and that was where she would always be.

Harlequin Presents®

Coming Next Month

Available in May wherever paperback books are sold, or through Harlequin Reader Service·

In the U.S.
901 Fuhrmann Blvd
P O. Box 1397
Buffalo, N.Y 14240-1397

In Canada
P.O Box 603
Fort Erie, Ontario
L2A 5X3

**In April, Harlequin brings you the
world's most popular romance author**

JANET DAILEY

No Quarter Asked

Out of print since 1974!

After the tragic death of her father, Stacy's world is shattered. She needs to get away by herself to sort things out. She leaves behind her boyfriend, Carter Price, who wants to marry her. However, as soon as she arrives at her rented cabin in Texas, Cord Harris, owner of a large ranch, seems determined to get her to leave. When Stacy has a fall and is injured, Cord reluctantly takes her to his own ranch. Unknown to Stacy, Carter's father has written to Cord and asked him to keep an eye on Stacy and try to convince her to return home. After a few weeks there, in spite of Cord's hateful treatment that involves her working as a ranch hand and the return of Lydia, his ex-fiancée, by the time Carter comes to escort her back, Stacy knows that she is in love with Cord and doesn't want to go.

**Watch for *Fiesta San Antonio* in July and
For Bitter or Worse in September.**

JDA-1

Have You Ever Wondered If You Could Write A Harlequin Novel?

Here's great news—Harlequin is offering a series of cassette tapes to help you do just that. Written by Harlequin editors, these tapes give practical advice on how to make your characters—and your story—come alive. There's a tape for each contemporary romance series Harlequin publishes.

Mail order only

All sales final

This April, don't miss Harlequin's new Award of
Excellence title from

elusive as the unicorn

*When Eve Eden discovered that Adam
Gardener, successful art entrepreneur, was
searching for the legendary English artist, The
Unicorn, she nervously shied away. The Unicorn's
true identity hit too close to home....*

*Besides, Eve was rattled by Adam's
mesmerizing presence, especially in the light
of the ridiculous coincidence of their names—
and his determination to take advantage of it!
But Eve was already engaged to marry her
longtime friend, Paul.*

*Yet Eve found herself troubled by the different
choices Adam and Paul presented. If only the
answer to her dilemma didn't keep eluding her....*

HP1258-1